W9-AGY-633

Usborne
Illustrated
Pirate
Stories

Usborne
Illustrated
Pirate
Stories

Illustrated by
Leo Broadley

Contents

Pirate of the Year

"Welcome to the Pirate of the Year contest!" Long John Silver shouted. The pirates standing around Shark-bite Cove let out a raucous cheer.

"This year's contestants are Merciless Meg, Sneaky Sal, Gormless Garry and..." Long John Silver stopped and stared at the tiny group of contestants in surprise. "Is that all?" he asked. "What about Billy Booty, or Blackheart?"

The crowd shuffled uncomfortably. The truth was, Merciless Meg had held the title for the last four years, and she was so, well, *merciless,* that nobody dared compete against her.

Just then a scrawny boy elbowed his way through the crowd. "I'll try," he said.

Long John Silver peered down at him. The lad barely came up to his knees. "And you are..?"

"Johnny Titch," the boy replied.

"Let's hear it for Little Johnny Titch!" shouted Long John Silver. Another cheer went up from the onlookers. Merciless Meg looked furious.

"Now remember the rules," said Long John Silver. "There are no rules! Har, har, har! But there are three stages to the competition: Treasure-Finding, Swashbuckling Swordsmanship and Pirate Insults. Cheating is expected. The winner keeps the treasure and gets a golden trophy. May the best pirate win."

Long John Silver handed out maps to the contestants, each with a different route to the buried treasure.

Meg was the first to set off. "See you later, sharkbait," she snarled.

Gormless Garry was next. After a quick glance at his map, he scrabbled up the rocks, Sneaky Sal following close behind. "What's the point in looking at a map when you can just follow someone else?" Titch heard her mutter.

Titch's map led him around the coast to a thundering waterfall. An arrow on the map pointed up. "Right," said Titch. "Here goes." He grabbed hold of a dangling vine, which hung from the cliffs beside the waterfall, and started to climb.

"Ha!" came a voice from above. "You're a goner, tiresome Titch!" It was Merciless Meg, a dagger flashing in her hand.

"No!" cried Titch, but it was no use. Meg sliced through his vine and down he fell, into the freezing water below.

Titch surfaced, gasping for air, and scrambled out of the pool. There was no sign of Meg, so he began to climb another vine. When he finally reached the cliff top he spotted Meg up ahead. She was clutching her sides, laughing at something thrashing around in a bog. As Titch raced closer, he realized it was Sneaky Sal. "Help!" she wailed, "I didn't know it was sinking sand. I'm going under!"

"Serves you right for not looking at your map," snorted Meg. Using Sal's head as a stepping stone, she leaped to the other side.

Rushing towards the sinking sand, Titch threw Sal the end of his belt just before she disappeared beneath the surface.

"Thanks," she croaked as he hauled her to safety. Once ashore, Sal collapsed in a sticky, sandy heap on the grass. "Hurry," she panted. "The others are way ahead."

Titch found Garry in a grove, digging a deep hole, while Merciless Meg pelted him with coconuts.

"I've found the treasure!" Garry yelled triumphantly. "Oh!" he added, a moment later. "I can't get out of the hole."

"Push the treasure up first," said Meg, with a sly grin. "Then we'll help you out."

The treasure chest appeared at the top of the hole. "Fool!" chortled Merciless Meg. She wrenched the chest from Garry's grip and staggered off with it down the hill.

"But what about me?" Garry wailed.

"Don't worry," said Titch. He broke off the branch of a palm tree and lowered it into the hole. "You can use that to climb out," Titch called as he hurried after Meg.

Too late! As he raced into the cove, Meg was hauling the treasure chest across the finish line. "Meg is the winner of the first round! One point to Meg," announced Long John Silver.

"The next stage of the contest, Swashbuckling Swordsmanship, will be held aboard *The Sinking Seasnake*," he continued, pointing to a leaky-looking ship in the cove.

Sneaky Sal was too covered in sticky sinking sand to compete, but Gormless

Garry had crawled out of his hole and was determined to win back the treasure. So the three remaining contestants climbed onto the ship.

"Ready? GO!" boomed Long John Silver, and the three drew their cutlasses. Merciless Meg took one look at tiny Titch and smirked. "I'll deal with you in a minute," she said, and turned to Gormless Garry, slicing through the air with her blade.

Under Meg's ferocious attack, Garry was forced backwards onto the rigging. He scrambled higher and higher as he fended off her vicious blows. "You can't escape me," mocked Meg, clambering onto a pile of barrels. The next moment, she was hacking

Pirate of the Year

at the rigging.

As she cut through the ropes, the rigging sprang loose, swinging Gormless Garry over the edge of the ship. "Help!" he cried, clinging on with one hand and eyeing the water below.

Titch knew this was his chance. He dashed over to the pile of barrels and sliced through a rope holding them together.

"Waaaaaargh!" yelled Merciless Meg as the barrels began to roll out from under her. She did a merry dance on top of them, trying to keep her balance, but then went tumbling overboard and... SPLOSH!

"Thanks, Titch!" cried Garry, still dangling from one hand. "Now I only have you to deal with."

"I bet you're longing to get your hands on that treasure..." said Titch, with an innocent smile. "And the trophy too."

Garry's eyes lit up. "I am," he said.

"How big is the trophy anyway?" Titch asked.

"Oooh, about this big," said Garry, letting go of the rigging to gesture with both hands. "Argh!" And down he went too, into the deep blue sea.

The crowd went wild. Merciless Meg and Gormless Garry crawled onto the beach, as Long John Silver announced, "One point for Little Johnny Titch. Garry and Sal are out of the contest with no points. So it's neck and neck between Meg and Titch for the final round: Pirate Insults."

Titch and Meg faced each other on the beach. The crowd watched Titch doubtfully. He'd done well so far, but could he insult Meg badly enough to win?

"Go!" boomed Long John Silver.

Meg narrowed her eyes, "Weedy prawn."

Titch shrugged. "Scurvy seawitch."

"Measly, stinking scragglefish."

"Wrinkly, crooked old seahag."

"Jelly-boned spawn of a blithering bilgebuster."

"Ooooh," the crowd murmured, turning to look at Titch expectantly. How would he follow that?

"Ruthless scum of the seabottom," he ventured. The crowd groaned, and Meg's eyes gleamed. She had the upper hand.

"Scurvy, scurrilous, lily-livered, blubbering drivelswigger!" she said triumphantly.

The crowd applauded, and Titch eyed her tensely. Meg was evil, ruthless and black-hearted. But that's exactly how she wanted to be seen. The worst insults just weren't insulting to her. Suddenly Titch grinned. He knew what the biggest insult to Meg would be.

"Merciless Meg," he said sweetly, "You are a delightful, pretty darling of a sugar-plum fairy."

Meg gasped and went white. "Am not!" she whispered. The crowd went quiet.

"A delicate syrup-sweet princess," Titch said.

Meg staggered backwards. "No..."

"The cutest little pompom of a dainty doll," said Titch, delivering his final thrust.

Meg's face turned scarlet and then green, and she keeled over in a dead faint.

There was a stunned hush from the crowd. And then laughter erupted. "I've never heard a more insulting insult," Long John Silver declared, shaking his head in wonder. He grabbed Titch's arm and held it aloft. "We have a champion," he announced to the crowd.

"The Pirate of the Year is Little Johnny Titch! Hereafter to be known as

Terrible-Tongued Titch!"

Cheers echoed out over the open sea, and the celebrations went on for a week. Merciless Meg kept a very low profile. And, after that, every time she encountered Terrible-Tongued Titch, Meg turned a little green and headed away from him as fast as her ship would carry her.

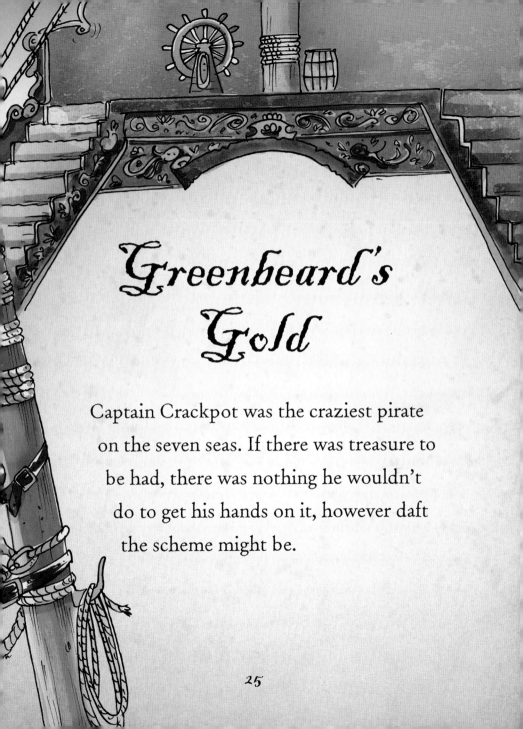

Greenbeard's Gold

Captain Crackpot was the craziest pirate
on the seven seas. If there was treasure to
be had, there was nothing he wouldn't
do to get his hands on it, however daft
the scheme might be.

One sunny morning, he strode across the deck of *The Barking Dogfish* with a wild-eyed smile spread across his face.

"Wake up, you lazy clams!" he boomed at his crew, waving a tattered scrap of paper above his head.

"What's he up to now?" yawned Joe Bones, clambering out of his hammock.

"It's bound to be another harebrained scheme," Sally Patch replied.

"Gather around, you dozy flounders," bellowed Crackpot. "And cast your scurvy eyes on this little beauty."

The crew cautiously gathered around their captain.

"I won it last night," explained Crackpot,

laying the paper on the deck. "There was a 'Sing-Along Sea Shanty Contest' at the Spyglass Inn, and Greenbeard's treasure map was the first prize."

The crew had all heard of Greenbeard. A year ago, he'd stolen a fortune in gold doubloons from a merchant ship. He was captured shortly afterwards, but no one knew what had become of the treasure.

The crew had to admit the map showed more promise than Crackpot's usual loony plots – like his attempt to sneak aboard a merchant ship disguised as a cat. Or the time he tried to steal the King of Spain's crown while he was still wearing it.

"Set a course for Black Island!" Crackpot

ordered Barney, the first mate. "Hoist every
sail we've got and we'll be there by tea time."

The thought of gold spurred on the crew,
and by early afternoon Black Island was in
sight. But the shoreline was too rocky to
bring the ship in close.

"Think of all that lovely booty, waiting
to be dug up," cried Crackpot. "Last one
in's a periwinkle!" With that, he dived off
the ship and swam towards the island.

But before he could reach the shore,
he heard the frantic cries of his crew back
on deck.

Crackpot craned his neck in their
direction. "What are you squawking about,
you mangy lot?" he yelled.

"Look out!" warned Sally.

"Dead ahead!" yelped Joe.

The captain looked back towards the island and gulped. Carving its way through the surf was a silvery shark's fin.

Arms and legs thrashing furiously, Crackpot turned and swam back to his ship.

He stood dripping on deck, glowering at the shark gliding menacingly back and forth along the shoreline.

"No shark is getting between me and that treasure," spluttered the captain, spitting out a clump of seaweed. "Lower the lifeboat!"

Soon Crackpot and his crew were rowing across to the island.

"I can almost smell those lovely doubloons!" murmured Crackpot.

But he'd spoken too soon. There was an ear-splitting crunch, and the pirates watched in horror as a chunk of the boat disappeared beneath them, to be replaced by a shark with a grinning mouthful of wood. "Help!" screamed Barney.

"Swim for it!" hollered Sally.

"Well, that's that, I suppose," sighed Joe, as they heaved themselves back onto their ship.

"We'll never get past that shark," agreed Barney.

"Bilge wash!" snorted Crackpot. "I didn't get to be a pirate captain by giving in to an overgrown sardine."

He scuttled down to the ship's workshop. For the next hour, the air was filled with bangs and crashes. Finally, the captain emerged, staggering under a pile of old junk.

"I knew the rubber we stole from that last merchant ship would come in useful," he grinned.

He tied two tall wooden posts to the side of the ship. Then he attached a long strip of rubber between them. Straining and sweating, he hauled the rubber across the deck until it was taut, and fastened it to the side with thick rope.

"What do you think, shipmates?" he said proudly.

"Erm, what is it?" asked Barney.

"It's a catapult, you crab cake," replied Crackpot, leaning back on the giant rubber band.

"You're not going to..?" began Joe.

"How will you get back?" called Sally.

But Crackpot ignored her. He swung down his cutlass and sliced through the rope.

There was a loud twang, and he shot into the air.

"Wooooaaaah!" yelled Crackpot. Seconds later, he came down with a thud on the shore of Black Island.

"Ha, ha!" laughed Crackpot delightedly, spitting out a mouthful of sand. "Next stop, Greenbeard's Gold."

He pulled the map from his pocket and checked the directions.

"Forty paces due north," he muttered, striding across the sand. "Fifty paces east, sixty paces north, twenty paces west... ah, this is the spot!"

He thrust his shovel into the ground and began digging.

It was hard work. "I should have told that load of lazy weevils to follow me over," grumbled Crackpot.

There was a nerve-jangling thud as his shovel hit something hard. A moment later, he was scraping earth from a wooden chest.

A shot from his pistol made short work of the chest's padlock. Crackpot eagerly tugged open the lid and his face was bathed in a golden glow.

He shoved his hands into the chest and let hundreds of glittering coins trickle through his fingers.

"We're rich!" shouted Crackpot. "No one will ever call me crazy again. Just wait till my crew sees..."

Suddenly he recalled what Sally had said as he left. How was he going to get back to the ship? There was no rubber on the island to build a catapult. And there was a hungry shark between him and *The Barking Dogfish.*

"Hmmm..." thought Crackpot, mulling over an idea. "It's crazy, but it might just work." He lifted the chest from the hole and carried it down to the beach.

"First, a spot of fishing," said Crackpot. He got to work with a long branch, a vine and a worm. In no time, he'd caught a fat, juicy fish.

Next, he built a raft and put the chest on top. He pushed the raft into the water and climbed aboard.

"Now let's see if this works..." chuckled Crackpot, waving the fish in the air.

Sure enough, the hungry shark leaped from the water and tried to snap up the fish.

Back on *The Barking Dogfish,* Joe Bones

scratched his head. "What's Crackpot up to?" he wondered, passing his telescope to Sally. "Has he gone stark, staring crazy?"

"Actually," replied Sally, "he could well be a crazy genius."

Using another vine, Captain Crackpot had lassoed the unsuspecting shark.

Still straining to reach the fish, the shark swam away from the beach, pulling Crackpot and his raft through the water.

"Yahoo!" yelled Crackpot, as he zoomed across the waves.

"Good old Crackpot!" laughed Joe.

"I told you he was a genius," chuckled Sally.

"Ahoy there, maties!" shouted Crackpot,

Greenbeard's Gold

as he reached the ship. "How do you like my shark-powered raft?"

The captain let go of the lasso and flung the fish far out to sea. As the hungry shark swam after it, Crackpot hurled the treasure chest onto the ship and clambered aboard.

Moments later, the captain was sharing out the gold among his crew.

"Three cheers for Captain Crackpot!" cried Joe.

"Don't you mean Captain *Jackpot?*" said the captain with a grin.

The Battle of Toasted Cheese

Captain Pugh gazed sadly at his dinner – a
plate of stale ship's biscuits. "It's not
enough for a hungry pirate," he moaned.
"I'll starve if I don't get some proper food
soon. And they're riddled with weevils!" he
added, pointing to a mass of small brown
beetles crawling in the crumbs.

41

"Nice and crunchy though," put in Jem, the first mate, helpfully.

"Urgh!" said Pugh, rubbing his stomach. There was a loud gurgling sound. "How can I terrorize people with a tummy rumble?" he complained.

"But there isn't anyone to terrorize," Jem pointed out. It was true. It had been weeks since they'd come across any other ships, and supplies were running low.

"Ship ahoy!" called the lookout. "A merchant ship, loaded down and low in the water. I think we're in luck!"

"Just in time," Pugh chuckled. "Get ready, lads, grab your weapons! It's time to steal us some grub."

Across the water on *The Saucy Sal*, a rich smell of cheese filled the air. Below decks, the ship was crammed with the stuff. Big cheeses. Small cheeses. Round cheeses. Hard cheeses. Smelly cheeses. Wax-coated cheeses. Cheeses, cheeses and more cheeses.

Ned Finn, the *Sal*'s captain, was staring moodily at his navigation chart. "We've been blown off course," he sighed. "Now we're in pirate waters!"

"That's all right, we've got plenty of cannons..." began Bosun Sid.

"But no cannon *balls!*" interrupted Ned. "We should have taken on more supplies and left some of these blasted cheeses behind. We'll just have to hope we don't run into any other ships..."

"Too late," said Sid, glancing up. "There's one approaching now!"

Ned pulled out his telescope. A lean, mean-looking ship was racing towards them, a red flag fluttering ominously from its mast.

"I know that flag," he said, frowning. "It's Peg-leg Pugh. And we don't have any ammunition! What can we do?"

Sid thought about the cheeses stacked

everywhere. Some of them were just the size of cannon balls, and almost as hard. "I have an idea..."

The ships drew closer. The two captains eyed each other up through their telescopes and gave their orders.

"Broadside attack," snapped Pugh. "Cutlasses at the ready!"

"Stay back," called Ned. "Load the cannons, but don't fire yet. Does everyone have their cheeses?"

His crew nodded. A row of cannons lined the deck, each with a pile of cheeses beside it, instead of cannon balls.

"I hope this works," thought Sid. He had no idea what would happen when cheese met exploding gunpowder. Would it melt into a sticky mess, or would it blast out of the cannons like real ammunition? "We'll find out soon enough," he sighed.

The gap between the ships was closing. Now they could see Pugh and his crew, scowling and waving their weapons. They were a fierce, hungry-looking bunch.

"Ready, aim, FIRE!" yelled Ned.

The crew of the *Sal* covered their ears.

BANG! BANG! BANG! A storm of cheeses flew across the water. The air filled with a delicious smell of toasted cheese.

On the pirate ship, Pugh and his crew raced around in confusion, trying to get out of the way... SPLAT! SPLAT! SPLAT!

The Battle of Toasted Cheese

The cheeses hit the deck. But instead of punching holes through it, they collapsed into soft yellow puddles.

"Uh-oh," thought Sid, watching through his telescope. "They've gone all melty – not like real cannonballs at all. The pirates will know we haven't got any real ammo. We're doomed!" In despair, he lowered his telescope, crossed his fingers and waited for the attack to start.

To his surprise, nothing happened. Cautiously, he uncrossed his fingers. "What's going on?" he demanded.

Ned had been watching the other ship. He laughed. "Take a look yourself!"

Sid peered into his telescope. The pirates

had dropped their weapons and were bending down, scrabbling at the puddles... "They seem to be eating the cheese!" he exclaimed. And they were.

It was the best meal the pirates had had in weeks. "This is delicious," said Jem with his mouth full, spraying crumbs everywhere. "Perfect with ship's biscuits."

Pugh nodded happily, cheese dripping from his fingers. "I love toasted cheese," he sighed, scooping up another gloopy lump. "And we didn't even have to fight for it!"

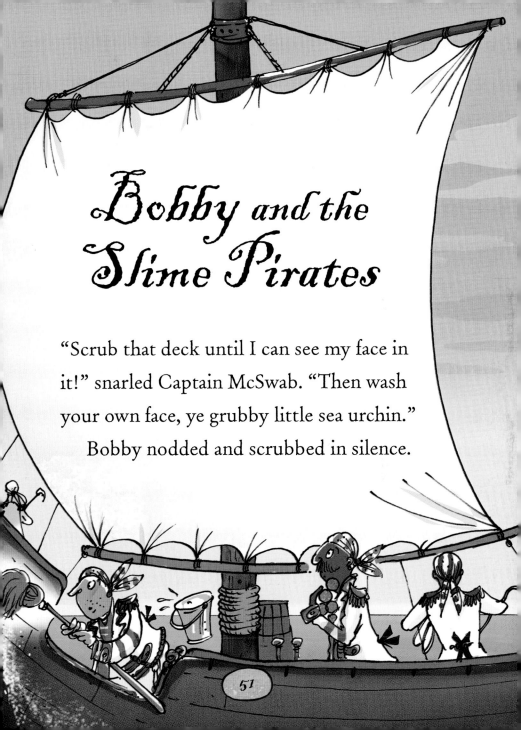

Bobby and the Slime Pirates

"Scrub that deck until I can see my face in it!" snarled Captain McSwab. "Then wash your own face, ye grubby little sea urchin." Bobby nodded and scrubbed in silence.

"I want this ship to shine for when I catch up with those Slime Pirates," said Captain McSwab. "The day I sink those scabby scruffs will be the finest day of my life."

As the captain strode away in his spotless white pirate suit, Bobby sighed. "This is *so* unfair," he thought. "When I ran away to sea to become a pirate, I thought my life would be full of adventure and danger. But I haven't even fired a cannon or seen a single treasure chest." In fact, the closest Bobby had come to treasure was the captain's gold tooth, right at the back of his mouth (yuck).

"I've joined the least piratey pirate crew in the world. All I do is clean, clean, clean." He looked down at his to-do list from the captain:

Wash the crew's socks (that's 99 in all, as Cook has a wooden leg)

Polish my boots

Wash Razorclaws

Scrub all the hammocks

Polish my gold tooth until it gleams

Wash 50 pairs of pirate underpants

Wash the scrubbing brush you used to wash the 50 pairs of pirate underpants

Wash it again, just to be sure it's clean

And it went on like that for five more
pages. By bedtime, Bobby was so tired, he
could barely crawl into his (spotless)
hammock. But as he drifted off, there was a
shout: "Enemy ship to starboard, Cap'n."

"The Slime Pirates!" cried the captain.
"Those dirty sea dogs. Ha! Now's my
chance to be rid of 'em once and for all."

Bobby leaped out of his hammock.
Excitement at last! He'd heard about the
Slime Pirates – whispered stories of grimy
pirates who were always coated in a thin
layer of slime thanks to the sea monsters
they kept as pets. He'd always wanted to see
the Slime Pirates in the flesh.

And there they were, in a black and

stinky ship, dripping with revolting goo.
The captain was a bold woman whose hair
stood stiff with dirt. She was
covered in so much sea
monster gunk, that even her
face gleamed green.

Just before the Slime Pirates
swung across to board *The Shiny
Tuppence,* there was a furious
BOOM! Captain McSwab was
firing the cannons. BOOM!
The next cannonball tore a
huge hole in the enemy ship and it swiftly
sank beneath the waves.

"Ha!" laughed Captain McSwab in
triumph. "May the ocean wash you clean,

you filthy varmints. I've got those grimy greaseballs at LAST!"

The slime pirates were splashing around in the sea, blinking in surprise.

The captain cheered again, then threw a cloth at Bobby.

"Now polish those cannons," he ordered.

As the captain stalked off to celebrate with a soapy bath, Bobby got to work. But he was so exhausted, that he fell asleep draped over one of the cannons.

He awoke to find a rough hand stealing over his mouth. He tried to cry out but another arm grabbed him from behind and shoved him into a scratchy, smelly sack. In fact, the smell was so disgusting, he fainted.

When he came to, Bobby was on his back on a beach, staring up at a circle of dirty, slime-coated faces.

"You're the Slime Pirates!" cried Bobby.

"Aye. And I'm Captain Gunge. Pleased to meet you, boy."

"My name's not boy, it's Bobby," said Bobby. He was too annoyed to be scared. "And I'm *not* pleased. You stuffed me in a sack and kidnapped me. A really, really smelly sack!"

Captain Gunge laughed, a great big, noisy laugh that shook slime from her skin and dirt from her hair. "I like you," she said. "The thing is, we needed a cabin boy, so we stole you. That's what Slime Pirates do: we steal whatever isn't nailed to the decks." She grinned, showing black teeth.

Bobby had to admit that's why he'd gone to sea – to be a *real* pirate. "But why should I trust you?" he said.

"You shouldn't. We're a crew of scurvy sea dogs," said Captain Gunge. "But, if you join us, we can show you more marvels in one day than you've seen in your short life."

Bobby folded his arms. "Prove it. You don't even have a ship anymore."

"We have something better." Captain Gunge turned to her crew. "Sing the Summoning Song, me hearties!"

The Slime Pirates began to sing. Their voices were as sweet as their breath was foul:

We call upon the monsters,

The slime-fiends of the deep:

Rise up, rise up and join us,

We wake you from your sleep.

As the pirates stopped singing, the sea began to ripple. Then the ripples turned into waves, crashing down on the beach.

A dozen slimy heads rose out of the water. The monsters stretched up their long, long necks and their teeth, sharp as knives, flashed in the sunlight. Each beast had long waggling tentacles that oozed with slime.

"Sea monsters!" cried Bobby. "So the legends are true? Do you really ride them?"

Captain Gunge just smiled and waved to the creatures. The sea beasts waved their

tentacles in return. "GROAR!" they growled as one.

The slime-coated captain leaped onto the back of the nearest monster. She held out her hand to Bobby. "Would you care to join us for a ride? I've a bone to pick with Captain McSwab."

Bobby took her hand and Captain Gunge pulled him up behind her. She patted the creature's flank as the other pirates leaped onto their mounts. "OK, Slimebelly? Ready to go? Make for *The Shiny Tuppence!*"

Slimebelly the sea monster roared in agreement and sped towards *The Shiny Tuppence*, powering through the water with its churning tentacles. The other slime pirates

Bobby and the Slime Pirates

followed on their own monstrous mounts.

Bobby whooped with joy as they rushed through the water. "I could get used to this," he cried. *The Shiny Tuppence* was not far ahead now. Bobby saw Captain McSwab on the deck.

"ARGH! Sea monsters!" he shrieked, leaping back in surprise. "Get away from my ship, you dirty creatures."

"No chance!" cried Captain Gunge. "Board 'er, lads!"

The pirates jumped from their sea monsters onto the ship, surrounding Captain McSwab and his pristine pirates.

"Now," said Captain Gunge. "Let's see if we can coat this entire ship with oozing, slobbery slime, shall we?"

The Slime Pirates cheered and the sea monsters grinned. A moment later, they were squirting great blobs of green goo from their tentacles.

"Please, call them off," whimpered Captain McSwab. "They're getting slime all over the rigging. Their filthy tentacles are getting gloop on my gunwale. Yuck! Make them stop, I'm begging you!"

Captain Gunge thought about it for a moment. "Are you really sure you *want* a

ship?" she said at last. "I
mean, you're terrible at
being a pirate. All you want to
do is keep things clean and tidy. Why not
move to a nice, spotless desert
island instead?"

Captain McSwab looked
shocked. "I... I... never thought of that
before," he stammered.

"Well, the nearest island's ten minutes'
swim that way," said Captain Gunge,
pointing back to the island they'd just come
from. "Go, or I'll get Slimebelly here to give
you a great big gunky kiss."

Her sea monster craned its neck closer to
Captain McSwab, trailing goo in its wake.

Captain McSwab jumped screaming into the sea. His shining-white crewmates weren't far behind.

Captain Gunge turned to Bobby. "So, will you be my cabin boy? You're a brilliant sea-monster rider, and you already know this ship."

Bobby thought for a moment. "I don't have to *clean* anything, do I?"

"What do you think?" asked Captain Gunge, grinning her filthy black teeth.

"Will we go on adventures, looking for treasure and stuff?" Bobby added.

"Why do you think we're all so mucky? We're too busy looking for treasure to wash," said Captain Gunge.

She clapped him on the back. It left a sticky mark behind. Bobby smiled. He was a real, disgusting, dirty, treasure-seeking pirate at last.

Gone

Captain Lester was so angry that he couldn't speak. He pointed at the empty space on the dock and made furious spluttering sounds. *Where was his ship?*

69

"I think it's gone, sir," observed Big Maud – the tallest pirate on the crew.

The pirates of *The Crumpled Sausage* were not imaginative when it came to nicknames. As a general rule, they had roughly one brain cell each. Big Maud was unusual. She had two.

"I know it's gone!" yelled Captain Lester. "I can see it's gone!"

"I thought you might not have noticed," said Big Maud. "You went all quiet, except for those funny spluttering noises."

"Grrrr!" fumed the captain. "You just stick to your usual job of hitting enemies with heavy objects, will you?"

Big Maud looked around. "But there's no

one to hit," she pointed out. "So, how are we going to find our ship?"

"Hmm..." said the captain.

Big Maud waited. And waited. But the captain did not appear to have a cunning plan up his sleeve. Or any plan at all.

Big Maud scrunched up her face and thought as hard as she could. Finally, she said, "We could go and ask some questions around the island, see if we can find any clues about where the ship's gone?"

"Of COURSE I'm going to do THAT," snapped Captain Lester. "I was just about to say that before you interrupted. What kind of fool do you think I am?"

Big Maud said nothing.

"Let's go!" said Captain Lester.

First, they went to the Merry Mermaid Inn, where all the pirates stayed when they were on shore.

Captain Lester stood on a table. "Has anyone seen my ship? It's big and made of wood and it's MINE!" he bellowed.

The pirates in the inn all stared blankly at him.

Big Maud tapped him on the shoulder – she could do it easily, even when he was standing on a table. "Maybe you should tell them what it looks like, sir?"

"I was about to!" the captain humphed. Then, louder, he added, "It's got black sails and a red pirate flag. Anyone seen it?"

The pirates at the inn all shrugged.

"Pah! You lot are about as much use as a lead lifeboat." Captain Lester turned to Big Maud. "Come on, let's go and try our luck elsewhere."

As they left the inn, a little girl came running up to them. She looked at the captain and smiled.

"Hello," she said. "I'm Maria McReed and I can help you find your ship... but only if you give me a gold doubloon and let me join your crew. I think I'd make an excellent pirate," she added.

Big Maud frowned. There was something fishy about all this, and it wasn't just the captain's usual smell. A small child couldn't have stolen their ship though... could she?

Captain Lester didn't share Maud's suspicion. He couldn't stop laughing. "If *you* can find my ship... hahahahaha... Well, if you do, not only will I give you a whole chest of gold, I'll make YOU the captain and I'll be

your cabin boy! Hahahaha! The very idea!"

"Sir, are you sure it's wise to offer that?" asked Big Maud. "What if she succeeds?"

Captain Lester was still laughing. "Har, har! The very idea! A tiny child like that, find MY ship?"

"You have a deal," said Maria, who didn't seem to mind being laughed at. "I'll be your captain and take your gold for my own – just as soon as I find your ship." She held out her palm. "I need the doubloon first, though."

Captain Lester flipped her the gold coin, still chuckling. The little girl grabbed it and ran away.

"I don't think we're going to see that coin again," said Big Maud, glumly. "Mind you, I don't suppose a single doubloon will make much difference when we've lost a whole ship."

Captain Lester stopped laughing. "What if I never see my ship again?" he moaned.

Big Maud shrugged. "If we don't have a ship, then I suppose we won't be pirates any more. We'll just be a group of cutlass-wielding people in funny hats."

At that, Captain Lester burst into tears. Big Maud wished she'd kept quiet.

They slept the night at the Merry Mermaid Inn, not feeling very merry. But in the morning, as they were eating a breakfast of crunchy prawnflakes, Big Maud glanced out at the bay. "Look, Captain!" she cried.

The captain followed her gaze, and there, in the dock, was *The Crumpled Sausage*. Captain Lester, Big Maud and their shipmates rushed out, leaving their prawnflakes half-eaten, hardly believing their eyes.

A short, angry-looking man wearing a bright blue uniform, with a tidy beard and even tidier hair was standing in front of the boat. Little Maria McReed was standing beside him.

"How did you do it?" asked Captain Lester. "Who's this man? Is he the vicious varmint who stole our ship?"

The angry man snorted in disgust. "Stole? Nonsense. I was just doing my job." He produced a shiny badge from his pocket.

Everyone peered at it, but no one said anything.

"He's a Pirate Parking Inspector," explained Maria. "I paid your fine for you, and he brought your ship back."

The pirates of *The Crumpled Sausage* stared at her, slack-jawed.

"Didn't any of you lot see this?" The angry man in uniform pointed to a sign on the wall of the dock.

"We *saw* it," said Captain Lester. "We just couldn't, um, *read* it."

"None of us can read," added Big Maud.

Gone

"No one's ever taught us how. So, what does it say?"

"It says NO MOORING HERE OR WE WILL TOW YOUR SHIP AWAY. FINE: ONE DOUBLOON," said the Pirate Parking Inspector. "You moored there, so I towed your ship away. That's the rule."

"That's not fair!" said Captain Lester. "I didn't know."

"Not my problem," said the Pirate Parking Inspector. "I just work here." Then he nodded to Maria and stalked off looking for more pirates to fine.

Captain Lester turned to the little girl. "You knew what had happened to the ship, and you didn't tell me?"

Maria shrugged. "You didn't ask." She strode over to Captain Lester and drew his cutlass, swishing it in the air a few times.

"Oi!" complained Captain Lester. "You can't do that!"

"I can," said Maria. "I'm your captain."

"You did say she could be," agreed Big Maud. "If she found the ship."

"But... but..." said Captain Lester, helplessly.

The little girl walked up the gangplank onto the ship, then turned to address the crew of *The Crumpled Sausage*.

"I'm Captain McReed," she said. "And my first act as your captain will be to teach you to read, so you don't get into this kind of trouble again."

Big Maud smiled. Captain McReed was going to be a much better captain than Lester ever was.

And, by the stormy look on his face, Ex-captain Lester was going to be the grumpiest cabin boy on all the seven seas.

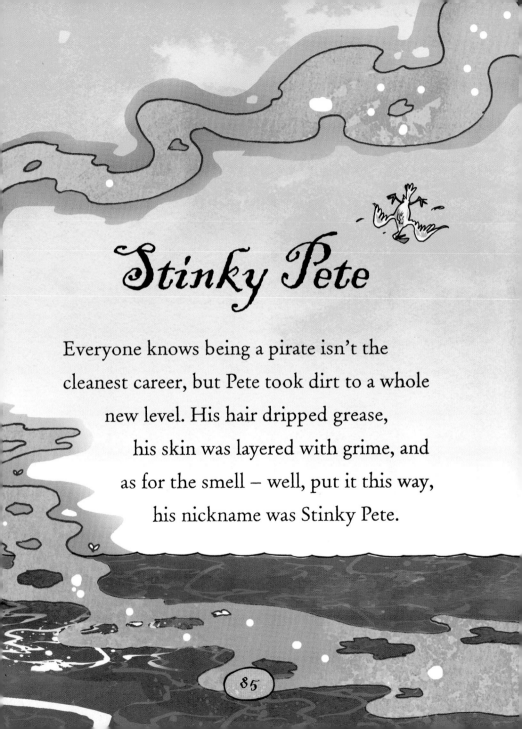

Stinky Pete

Everyone knows being a pirate isn't the
cleanest career, but Pete took dirt to a whole
new level. His hair dripped grease,
his skin was layered with grime, and
as for the smell – well, put it this way,
his nickname was Stinky Pete.

Stinky Pete

"I'd rather walk the plank than take a bath," Pete bragged. Everywhere he went, an overpowering stench of cheesy rotting socks went with him. What Pete didn't realize was that everyone could smell him coming... so he didn't get his hands on the loot very often.

One bright, breezy day, Pete was staring out to sea when he spotted a trim little pirate ship. Through his telescope, he could see the deck was stacked neatly with barrels. He grinned, imagining all the delicious things that might be inside.

"Ginger beer, pickled herrings, sugared plums, rum bumbo... This might just be my lucky day!" He changed course at once.

Crafty Kate and her crew didn't notice

Pete until it was too late.

"Ship - *achoo!*" sneezed the first mate. "I mean, ship ahoy!" he said crossly, as the dirty-looking ship bore down on them.

"Drat this cold," sniffed Kate. "It's Stinky Bete. I didn't even sbell hib cobing." She blew her nose on her sleeve, then gave a crafty grin. "I've got an idea..."

By the time Pete leaped aboard, Kate was leaning nonchalantly against a huge barrel.

"Give me your cargo!" bellowed Pete. For a moment, Kate was glad of her stuffy nose. She knew that otherwise she'd be knocked out by his foul-smelling breath.

"Certainly," she said. "Here, catch!" And she gave the barrel, which was lying on its side, a push. Immediately it began to roll, gathering speed as it went...

"Aargh!" screamed Pete, as the barrel thundered towards him. There was nowhere to go except... He hesitated, then took the plunge. *Splash!* A moment later, he was in the sea. *SPLOSH!* The barrel hit the water beside him.

Crafty Kate raced to the side of her boat and looked over.

The barrel was bobbing in the waves, pink bubbles seeping out between its cracks. Stinky Pete surfaced right in the middle of the froth. He pushed his dripping hair out of his eyes and looked around in astonishment.

Stinky Pete

"Wh-what's happening?" he stuttered. "The water's gone all pink!"

Pete looked different too. His hair gleamed and his skin shone. And as for the smell... He sniffed the water. "Roses?"

Kate snorted with glee. "Rose bathsalts," she said. "That'll teach you to come after me, Stinky Pete."

The whole crew fell about laughing.

Pete turned pinker than the water with embarrassment. "I smell like a perfumed princess," he wailed. "I'll be a laughing stock!"

"You know, you should really thank me," called Kate as she sailed away. "Now you don't smell so bad, it should be easier being a pirate."

To his surprise, Pete discovered Crafty Kate was right. Without his stink, he was much better at creeping up on other ships – and 'Perfume Pete' soon became the terror of the seas.

The Pirate Parrot

Bella longed to be a pirate. She had the hat and the shiny cutlass... She even had a parrot named Feathers, who loved screeching pirate phrases. *Pieces of eight! Shiver me timbers! Who's a scurvy sea dog?*

During the day, Bella dreamed about swashbuckling swordfights. At night, she counted imaginary bags of treasure while she fell asleep. So when she spotted a Jolly Roger fluttering from an unfamiliar ship, she raced down to the quayside.

The pirate captain cast a surly glance at her. "Whaddyerwant?" he growled.

"To join your crew!" said Bella, in her gruffest, most piratey voice.

"A pirate's life for me!" squawked Feathers.

The captain clutched his sides and let out a deep guffaw.

"Erm... are you all right?" asked Bella nervously.

"Fine, fine," chuckled the captain. "It's

just, a scrap of a girl like you, wanting to be a pirate... and a talking parrot... har, har, har!"

"I've got my own hat," Bella said stubbornly. "And I know how to use a cutlass!"

The captain scratched his wild red hair. "We-ell, we could use someone to swab the decks," he admitted. "Our last cabin boy got so seasick he quit."

Bella grinned.

She grinned slightly less the next day, when she discovered just how much swabbing there was to do, never mind scrubbing and polishing... "And when you've finished that, you can peel the potatoes," added the captain, whose name was Red Ron.

"This isn't how I imagined being a pirate," she muttered to Feathers across a mountain of muddy potatoes.

"Yo ho ho!" the parrot cackled back.

By nightfall, Bella was so tired she curled up in the hold on a pile of sacks, and fell fast asleep. Feathers tucked his head under a wing and slept too. So they didn't hear the oars splashing stealthily through the dark, or the rope thrown over the side of the ship... and neither did the rest of the crew, who were busy feasting and singing sea shanties in the captain's cabin.

Up on deck, cutlasses glinted wickedly in the moonlight. Cut-throat Jake and his gang of ruffians had climbed aboard, ready to...

"*Attack!*"

Red Ron's pirates grabbed their weapons, but they were too late. Jake and his ruffians' blades were at their necks.

"Now the treasure," crowed Jake. "Lock 'em up, lads, while we go looking for it!"

The commotion woke Bella. "What's going on?" she whispered to Feathers, listening to clumping footsteps and unfamiliar voices. "A raid?" She jumped up. "We'd better see what we can do..."

Light flickered in the doorway. Then Cut-throat Jake appeared, holding a sputtering candle. "In here!" he yelled. "Treasure's bound to be in the hold. Can any of you scurvy scallywags see any gold? I can't see further than my nose."

"Can't see anything in the dark," grumbled his gang, fumbling with more candles. Bella crept noiselessly over and, each time they struck a light, she blew it out.

"This is spooky," they muttered.

"What have we got here?" yelled Jake, rifling through boxes and barrels. "Salt pork, ship's biscuits..."

"Pieces of eight!" interrupted a loud voice from the back.

"Where?" asked Jake eagerly, staring into the shadows.

His gang looked at each other uneasily. "We didn't say anything, Cap'n."

"This is no time for jokes," snapped Jake. "I want that treasure!"

"Fifteen men on a dead man's chest," sang the voice. It was in front of them now.

"Stop singing and search," growled Jake.

"We *weren't* singing, Cap'n."

"So who was?"

His gang shuddered. "A g-g-ghost?"

Bella blew again... Jake's candle flickered

The Pirate Parrot

and went out, leaving the hold in total darkness. Now, with a flick of her wrist, she launched Feathers at the intruders...

Something soft brushed Jake's cheek. Then – from just overhead – there came a strange voice, chanting, "Dead men tell no tales..."

It was too much. Jake dropped his cutlass and ran back to his own boat, his gang close behind him. They didn't stop rowing until they were well away from the haunted ship.

Bella chuckled as the sound of oars and panicky shouts faded into the distance. Then she turned to Feathers. "Captain Ron and the crew must be locked up somewhere... Let's go and find them."

Red Ron bellowed with laughter when he heard how Bella and Feathers had frightened off Cutthroat Jake. "I don't think we'll be seeing any more of him," he said. He turned to Bella. "Good work, First Mate!"

Bella flushed. "*First Mate?*" That was second-in-command to the captain.

Red Ron nodded. "You deserve a promotion. And I'm making Feathers here the ship's mascot."

"Who's a clever pirate?" squawked Feathers.

"Not a clever pirate, a clever *parrot*,"

said Bella, proudly.

Feathers squawked again. "Yo ho ho and a bottle of rum," he sang.

"Just what I was thinking," said Red Ron. "It's time to celebrate!"

The Rotting Roger

As she sank beneath the waves, Betty Barnacle could still hear the battle raging above. But, as she was busy drowning, she wasn't really concentrating on it.

Her eyes dimmed and her chest felt as though it was bursting. As she sank to the very bottom of the sea, her last thought was, "I really should have ducked that cannonball..."

When Betty woke up on the sea bed, she realized that she wasn't breathing. "But I feel fine," she thought. "This is definitely peculiar."

Then, through the murky water, she saw someone swimming slowly towards her, wearing a long, ragged pirate coat, with a skull and crossbones sewn into the breast pocket.

As he came closer, she saw that his face was as wrinkled as a prune, and as pale as chalky dust. His eyes glinted red. "That pirate," thought Betty, "looks dead. Or dead-ish, given that he's doing the breast stroke."

Betty didn't scream. What was the point? It would make no sound underwater.

The strange man smiled – a surprisingly friendly smile. He pointed to the surface, and began to swim upwards. Betty followed him. Her limbs felt like lead anchors, but she managed to move slowly up... and up...

When they broke the surface, the pirate whistled, and someone threw them a rope. Before Betty knew it, she was being hauled on board a pirate ship.

Looking around at the ragged crew, she saw that every pirate had pale, wrinkled skin and glinting red eyes. Some had missing limbs or bony stumps. One even had a neat, circular hole in his chest, about the size of a cannonball.

"They're all dead," realized Betty.

"What *are* you?" she asked, staring at them in wonder. Then, remembering that she wasn't breathing herself, she added, "What am *I*?"

The pirate who'd brought her from the sea bed laughed a rattling laugh. "We're zombies, Ma'am. All who drown in this cursed stretch of sea come back to sail again. You're a zombie too, me hearty!"

Betty blinked. "Well," she thought. "I know a pirate's life is full of strange events, but I certainly didn't expect this when I got up this morning..."

The zombie pirate held out a hand for her to shake. "I'm Captain Guts, of *The Rotting Roger.* And you are?"

"I'm Betty. Betty Barnacle," she said, giving her firmest pirate handshake.

"Now we're all introduced, we'd better get going," said Captain Guts. "We've got work to do! If you care to join us, me hearty?"

"Aye, I do!" said Betty. She suspected that her old captain would run screaming if she tried to get her job back. "But what do zombie pirates *do*, exactly?"

"Do? We hunt for treasure of course," he said. "We might be dead, but we're still pirates. We just do our treasure hunting more slowly with a few more groaning noises."

The crew all groaned in agreement. "Arrrrrrrrrrrrrrrrrrrrrrgh," they said.

"Well, that's alright then." Betty felt relieved. She had been worried that she'd have to spend her days eating brains. She thought they would probably taste even worse than ship's biscuit. "So, which treasure are we going after today?" she asked.

The captain clicked his remaining fingers. "Set sail for Trelawny Bay," he cried. "I've heard that the finest gems and shiniest gold ever to grace a pirate's greedy eye are buried there, right in the middle of the island!"

"Aye aye, captain," said Betty, and she joined the rest of the crew to hoist the sails. *The Rotting Roger* flew across the waves for Trelawny Bay and treasure.

When they reached the shore, another boat was pulling in just ahead of them. The pirates on board were leaping down onto the sand and running for the middle of the island.

"Attack!" cried Captain Guts.

The crew looked worried. "But Captain, we're too slow!"

It was true. As the zombie pirates climbed out of the boat and started off across the sand behind the other crew, each step they took was painfully slow. "Our dead legs aren't as speedy as they used to be," complained Captain Guts.

Betty had to agree. She was walking as fast as she could, but she was still only moving at the pace of a lazy tortoise.

Captain Guts stomped his foot. "I can't believe this is happening again! Almost every time we go for some treasure, another crew gets there first! Curse our slow, dead legs!"

"Could we *scare* the treasure out of them?" suggested Betty.

"Good idea," said Captain Guts.

The zombie pirates lay in wait behind a large rock on the beach until the living pirates came out of the jungle, carrying the treasure.

"Charge!" cried Captain Guts. "Terrify them till they drop their treasure!"

The zombie pirates rose up from behind

the rock, growling, grimacing and making terrifying faces. Betty bared her teeth and moaned an unearthly moan.

"Aaaaaaaaargh!" cried the living pirates, running as fast as their legs could carry them, which was very fast indeed. But they held tight to the treasure.

The zombie pirates stared after them as they waded speedily through the shallows and back to their boat, still screaming.

"It's no good," said Captain Guts. "We can't compete with living pirates. If only there was more treasure just lying about, in places where normal pirates can't go..."

"But there is, Cap'n," said Betty. "I know of a place littered with fabulous treasure, where no mortal pirate can go."

Captain Guts beckoned her closer, and she whispered in his ear. A broad grin spread across his pruney face. "Back on board, me hearties!" cried the captain. "Set sail for Shipwreck Bay!"

The zombie pirates climbed slowly and creakily back on board *The Rotting Roger.*

When they reached Shipwreck Bay, the pirates anchored their boat. Then, one by one, they plopped into the sea and sank.

Betty peered down through the water until she saw what she was looking for. She beckoned to her crewmates, and they all dived down towards a shipwreck on the bottom of the sea. Swimming into the captain's cabin, she found a heavy chest that looked just right.

She pulled it open and, sure enough, it was full of gleaming gold and shining gems.

They spent the rest of the day exploring the bottom of the sea, and all the wrecked ships that lay there. "Living pirates couldn't survive more than a few minutes down here,"

thought Betty, happily, as she scooped up an armful of gems. "We have the sea bed to ourselves, to plunder as slowly as we like."

By the end of the day, they had a pile of treasure so big that it would take them a week to count it all.

"Well done, Betty," said the captain. "Living pirates might beat us on land..."

"But under the sea, the zombies rule!" finished Betty. She let out a joyful, gurgling shout and the other zombies cheered.

"Long unlive Captain Guts!" they cried.

"And long unlive Betty, the finest treasure-hunter on the crew!"

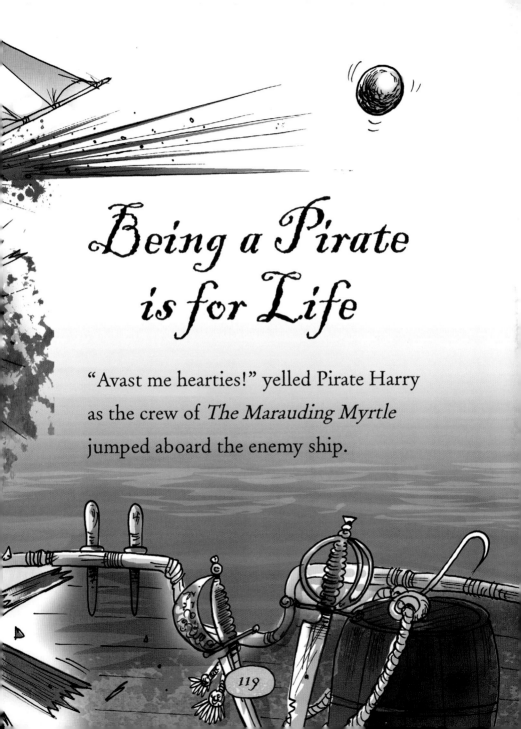

Being a Pirate is for Life

"Avast me hearties!" yelled Pirate Harry as the crew of *The Marauding Myrtle* jumped aboard the enemy ship.

Harry ran across the deck and into the nearest cabin. Dizzy with excitement, he discovered it was stuffed with sparkling, shimmering treasure.

He reached out and... Someone started shaking him and calling his name.

"Yes, Captain Bluebeard?" Harry mumbled, but it was his wife, Hilda.

"Harry! Wake up! You're dreaming. We haven't been on board *The Marauding Myrtle* for years."

"Oh! No..." said Harry, regretfully. He and his wife were retired pirates who lived a quiet life in a small house in Seatown. Harry sighed and tried to go back to sleep, hoping to dream of more pirate adventures.

The next morning, Harry sat at the
breakfast table looking
sadly at a slice of
burned toast.
After so many
years of eating
ship's biscuits,
Hilda had
never mastered
cooking in a

kitchen. Harry groaned. He was supposed
to mow the lawn today, but he really didn't
feel like it. He'd never had to think about
tending to a garden on board their old ship.

They had made some changes to the
house to make them feel more at home on

land. A large mast extended from the roof
and a ship's wheel stood proudly in the
lounge. But it wasn't enough for Harry. He
wanted to feel the rolling waves beneath him
and the wind in his hair. A house just wasn't
right for a pirate!

Harry was staring out of the window
wistfully when he spotted a flash of yellow
and blue on the horizon. He blinked in
surprise, but this time he definitely wasn't
dreaming. It was Captain Bluebeard's parrot,
flying towards them, with a message in the
bottle dangling from her beak.

"Hilda!" Harry cried. "Quick! Come
here! It's Polly. She's bringing us a message
from Bluebeard!"

As Polly landed on
the windowsill, Harry
uncorked the bottle,
took out the message
and began to read.

Me hearties Harry and Hilda,

Hope you are shipshape.
The Marauding Myrtle is in trouble!
Black Captain Jack has kidnapped Wilf,
our ship's boy. We need your help to
get him back. Let us know your answer
immediately.

Your old mate,

Captain Bluebeard

Harry's heart pounded with excitement.
This was their chance for one last adventure.

"No, no and no," said Hilda, after she had read the letter. "We're far too old to go back to sea."

"But Hilda! Captain Bluebeard needs us," pleaded Harry.

"How are you going to leap onto Captain Jack's ship with knees like yours?" Hilda continued.

She had a point, Harry admitted. But this was a personal request from Captain Bluebeard. They couldn't let him down. Harry had one more trick up his sleeve.

"You were the Dread Pirate Hilda, the most fearsome lady-pirate on the seas!" he exclaimed. "Men would quake in their boots at the very whiff of you. You've still got it, my beautiful barnacle!"

Hilda knew she shouldn't give in to such flattery. But she was tempted by the idea of beating the terrible Black Captain Jack once and for all.

"Alright then," she muttered. "I suppose we ought to help."

The next day, *The Marauding Myrtle* swept into port. Harry and Hilda made their way onto the ship (a little more slowly than before), as all the other pirates cheered.

"Welcome aboard, you senior scallywags!" cried Captain Bluebeard.

And with that they were off to the open seas. Harry was having the time of his life, and even Hilda was enjoying herself. "It's almost

like the good old days again,"
she admitted.

"Ship ahoy!" yelled the
first mate from the crow's nest
after two days of sailing. "It's
Black Captain Jack."

"The time has come, my
crumbly comrades," said
Captain Bluebeard. "Let's
get Wilf back from that dastardly dog."

The Marauding Myrtle sped for Captain
Jack's ship. Harry began to feel nervous.
Captain Jack was as dastardly a pirate as had
ever sailed the seas. What if he was too old
to take him on? What if Jack just laughed at
the sight of his white hair?

But the time for doubts was over. The crew of *The Marauding Myrtle* was jumping aboard Captain Jack's ship. Harry and Captain Bluebeard sped down the stairs, banging open doors left and right. They found Wilf in a tiny cabin at the very bottom of the ship.

"We've come to save you," Harry declared.

"Where's Captain Jack?" asked Wilf. "How will we ever get past him?"

"We'll find a way," said Harry, even though he wasn't sure exactly how.

They crept back up the stairs and onto the deck. There was no sign of Black Captain Jack – or Hilda, Harry realized. What if Jack had taken Hilda captive too?

"Aaaaaaaah!"

"What's that?" said Harry, as a cry echoed around the ship.

"It's coming from Captain Jack's cabin," said Wilf.

"Hilda!" Harry shouted, as the pirates rushed over to peer through the window.

Inside the cabin, Captain Jack was looming over Hilda. Harry ran to the door, but it was locked.

Then, he heard Captain Jack speak. "I r-remember you," he was stammering. "I sailed on your ship when I was a boy. You once m-made me scrape all the barnacles off the bottom of the boat with a toothpick because I s-stole a ship's biscuit!"

"And you're still just as naughty!" Hilda replied, wagging her finger at Captain Jack, who was shaking so much his knees knocked together. "How dare you kidnap Wilf from *my* pirate ship. Now, do you promise you'll never bother *The Marauding Myrtle* again?"

"Never!" Captain Jack's voice shook. He looked as if he'd just seen a ravenous shark that wanted him for dinner.

Hilda marched out of the cabin, with a shamefaced Captain Jack behind her.

"Wilf is free to go," Captain Jack said quietly to the assembled pirates.

"And?" a firm voice prompted.

Captain Jack looked as if he wanted to throw himself overboard. "And I'm very sorry

Wilf," he added.

The crew of *The Marauding Myrtle* cheered. Captain Bluebeard grinned. He had known all along that there was only one pirate who could frighten Captain Jack.

Back on board, Harry and Hilda were getting ready to go to sleep in their hammocks.

"I could get used to this," said Hilda sleepily. "I think you're right, Harry. A house just isn't right for us pirates. Being a pirate is for life!"

Do Not Light the Black Lantern

"An empty ship..." said Captain Avery.

He peered into his telescope, and his face turned pale. The crew of the pirate ship *Revenge* shuddered. The ship that sat in the moonlit bay was indeed empty.

"Sail us closer," the captain ordered.

At first, none of the crew moved. They stared at the empty ship and the island behind it, rocky cliffs topped with trees.

"Some say a dragon lives on that island," one of the pirates muttered. "Maybe it attacked that ship's crew."

The rest of the pirates mumbled in agreement. Every one of them wished they could simply sail past the island and the empty ship, leaving both far behind.

Except for one.

Jim, the ship's cabin boy, tried to push through the group for a better look. Rough hands shoved him away and he thumped to his backside on the deck.

Jim hated being a lowly cabin boy. He

hated scrubbing decks, pouring grog and polishing all the pirates' swords. He dreamed of being a real pirate, and this could be his chance.

The *Revenge* sailed closer to the empty ship. Moonlight glinted off the ship's brass rails. Swirls of mist floated like ghosts around the deck.

"Ahoy there!" called Captain Avery.

There was no reply.

"I need a volunteer to board that ship," the captain said and suddenly the pirates were seemingly hard at work, all far too busy to volunteer.

Only Jim stepped forward, raising his arm so high it hurt.

"Me!" he said. "Me! I'll go!"

"Good lad," the captain replied, slapping him on the back. "Lily-livered cowards!" he roared at the rest of the crew. "You've been shown up by the cabin boy."

The crew slid a plank from the *Revenge*, forming a wobbly bridge to the empty ship. As Jim climbed on, a shark circled in the dark water below. He'd never been so scared, or so excited.

Clouds covered the moon, and the night grew darker. Jim stepped onto the empty ship, his heart pounding like cannon fire. He unhooked a small lantern from the mast and struck the flint. His trembling hand caused the light to skitter around the deck.

"Hello?" he called.

Still no reply. A curtain of fog pulled back to reveal writing on the deck. Jim edged closer, holding the lantern low. A message was scratched on the wooden planks.

DO NOT LIGHT the BLACK LANTERN

Jim read the warning out loud. Then he turned and stared at the lantern shaking in his hand. The *black* lantern.

"It's the Curse of the Black Lantern!" one of the pirates shouted from the *Revenge*.

"No..." Jim gasped.

Every pirate knew the old tale. Whoever lit the black lantern was doomed.

"I'm sorry lad," called Captain Avery. "You cannot return to our ship."

Jim watched in horror as the *Revenge* sailed away through fading fog. He wanted to cry out, to beg them to return. But then a shadow fell over the ship...

He turned in time to see a huge wave rush closer. It slammed against the ship, washing Jim across the deck. Jim clung onto a rail, but another wave swept him over the side.

He plunged into the sea, and then rose, gasping. Fifty yards away, a shark's fin broke the water.

Jim swam frantically for the rocks.

Glancing back, he glimpsed the shark's
beady eyes and a row of razor
sharp teeth. He grasped
the rocks and dragged
himself from the
water, just as the
shark slid past.

He sat on the
rocks, shaking all
over from fear and
exhaustion. He was surprised to
see the black lantern beside him. It must
have caught in his shirt as he fell from the
ship. He was about to hurl it into the sea,
when he stopped. If he could get up higher,
maybe he could use the light to signal to a

passing ship.

He set off, slipping on wet rocks. The rocks grew into boulders, and the boulders rose into a cliff. Jim clipped the lantern to his belt and then began to climb. His arms strained and his fingers cut against cold, sharp stone. He heard a crash and looked up. An avalanche of rocks!

Jim pressed himself flat against the cliff, as dozens of rocks tumbled past, missing him only by inches. "The curse!" he groaned.

He pulled himself up onto the cliff top. Close by, pine trees swayed in the wind. From inside the woods, Jim heard a twig snap. Was someone there?

He crept between the trees. A few shafts of moonlight pierced the swaying branches, although it was too dark to see much. He struck the lantern's flint, but it was still wet and wouldn't light.

"Hello?" he called.

The only reply was the creak of the branches in the wind. Then Jim heard something else – a low rumbling noise. It sounded like an animal's snarl.

Something moved between shafts of

Do Not Light the Black Lantern

moonlight. Something fat and green and scaly and slimy...

"The dragon," Jim said, with a shudder.

A creature burst from the darkness. Ragged wings flapped and red eyes glared. Its mouth opened and blasted a jet of fire.

Jim dived to the ground. The flames roared over his head, crackling his hair. He scrambled up and staggered out of the woods. The dragon flew after him, smashing down trees. Smoke rose from its savage, snarling mouth.

Jim stumbled to the edge of the cliff. There was no escape. Unless...

In a flash, he realized how to rid himself of the curse. He slammed the black lantern onto a rock, and yelled to the dragon. "Come and get me!"

The beast rushed closer, spewing fire.

Jim ducked behind the boulder to shield himself from the flames.

The dragon roared. As it flew over the rock, its claw caught the black lantern and carried it away.

Jim cried out in delight. The beast's fiery breath had lit the lantern! Now the curse was on the dragon.

The dragon circled in the air, its roar growing even fiercer. It breathed another jet of fire, but a rush of wind blew the flames back at the creature's face.

The dragon's roar rose into a squeal as it

plummeted into
the sea. Steam
rose from the
water, and the
beast sank with
a sizzle.

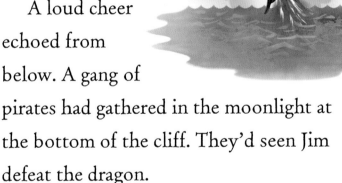

A loud cheer
echoed from
below. A gang of
pirates had gathered in the moonlight at
the bottom of the cliff. They'd seen Jim
defeat the dragon.

"You did it!" they cried. "You beat
the dragon."

They threw Jim a rope and he climbed
down to the shore.

"We've been stuck here for weeks," one of the pirates said. "None of us dared fight that creature."

Jim realized that this was the crew of the empty ship. "Did you abandon your ship after you found the black lantern on board?" he asked.

"We did," a pirate said. "We captured the ship from other sailors. But as soon as we discovered the black lantern, we knew we had to get as far from it as possible. Now we can return, and we could use a brave sailor like you."

"You mean as a cabin boy?" Jim asked.

The pirates all laughed. "No," said one, "as our captain."

Jim looked across the water, to where the dragon had disappeared, carrying the black lantern to the bottom of the sea. A wide grin spread across his face.

"So much for the curse," he thought. Lighting the Black Lantern was the best thing that had ever happened to him.

The Bookish Pirate

Lord Lummocks was bored. He was tired of talking to his clever friends, tired of reading clever books, and tired of giving clever speeches at parties. He was leafing through books in his library one day, when he found a picture of a fearsome-looking pirate.

"That's the life for me!" he declared. "A life of adventure on the open sea."

The next morning, he went down to the docks and paid a huge sum of money to have a ship built and stocked full of everything he might need, including hundreds of books on how to be a pirate. Then he put up a sign...

By Saturday, there was a scrappy band of pirates waiting for him on the docks.

"Good morning," chirped Lord Lummocks.

"Are you all here for the job?"

"Arrrrr..." the pirates growled.

He eyed the line. One man had a spoon for a hand. "Are you the cook?" Lummocks asked him.

The pirate nodded. "Spoon-hand Spencer's me name. I cook grub with or without weevils. If there's no grub, I can make bootstrap stew."

"Jolly good," beamed Lord Lummocks, not understanding a word. "And you," he said to a scar-faced horror of a man with no teeth. "Can you... um... Well, what sort of thing can you do?"

"'e can't chew for a start!" said a young boy loudly, and the scar-faced pirate took a swing at him. The boy ducked and said, "That's Scarface Stanley. He fought Blackbeard singlehandedly - that's where he got that scar. I'm Charlie the cabin boy. The others are Cutlass Carl, Stinky Sue, Kate Klinker and One-eyed Pete. Blackbeard sank the last ship we were on. He's a famous pirate captain, is Blackbeard..."

To avoid any further discussion, Lord Lummocks said, "You're all hired to start immediately. You'll be paid monthly."

Charlie frowned, "What about a share of the booty?"

"Don't you have your own boots?" asked Lord Lummocks, bewildered.

"Booty means treasure," snorted Charlie

in disbelief. "What kind of pirate captain doesn't know that?"

"Ah yes, all the treasure – um, booty – will be shared, of course," Lord Lummocks declared. "I'm Captain Lummocks. Welcome aboard my ship."

The band of pirates had been staring at him in astonishment. He seemed a very unlikely sort of pirate captain, but at the mention of treasure, they shrugged and trooped onto the brand new ship. "Blimey, landlubber. This is the shiniest ship I've ever seen," gasped Charlie.

"I had it specially made," said Lummocks.

"Pirates don't make ships, they steal 'em," grumbled Kate Klinker.

"We can always steal another one. Let's get going and find some treasure, shall we?" said Lummocks pleasantly. He stood at the helm and called, "Someone untie us then and we'll be off."

The crew looked at him blankly.

Charlie cleared his throat. "I think he means, 'Hoist the anchor and set sail. Quick about it, you scurvy seadogs!'" he explained.

The crew sprang into action. Within a few minutes, Lummocks and his pirate crew were sailing out to sea. They passed some rocky inlets, and Lummocks let out a shout, "Aha! Gentlemen! There's a likely-looking vessel over there!"

None of the crew batted an eyelid, until

Charlie helpfully yelled, "Ship ahoy!"

They squinted at the cliffs where, sure enough, a ship was emerging from a cove. Its ragged sails were black as night.

"It looks like a little one," said the captain. "It'll be an easy start!"

The crew burst out laughing.

"That ship only belongs to the most fearsome pirate to sail the seas," Charlie explained. "His name is—"

BOOOOOOM!!!

A cannonball burst through the side of Lummocks's ship onto the deck, leaving a great splintered hole behind it.

Lummocks spluttered, "I say, that's my new..." BOOOOM! Another cannonball burst onto the ship and knocked him off his feet. "Oof! Ouch my ankle!" he wailed as he hit the deck.

Before anyone could react, the black-sailed ship drew alongside them and the meanest, dirtiest, scowliest pirates imaginable started swinging aboard. "Make way, you stinking scoundrels," came a rumbling roar. The crowds of pirates parted to let through a terrifying figure.

A fearsome giant of a man strode forward, with a monstrous black beard wreathed in blue smoke that fizzed and curled about him in a most chilling way. His dark brows were

knitted together so tightly that his eyes could barely be seen. He opened his cavernous mouth and bellowed, "I'M BLACK—"

"—beard! Yes I know," Captain Lummocks interrupted gleefully. "I've read all about you. It's splendid to meet you in the flesh. You were my inspiration for becoming a pirate, you know. I always wanted to ask — how DO you do that thing with your beard? Is it really on fire?"

"ARGGGH!" roared Blackbeard, and all the pirates, even his own crew, shrank back.

"Simply terrifying," said Captain Lummocks cheerfully. "I would get up to shake your hand, but I'm afraid I've twisted my ankle."

"Lock him in his cabin!" Blackbeard thundered, and two pirates seized the captain and carried him away. "So kind," everyone heard him saying as he disappeared from view.

Blackbeard eyeballed the motley crew. "From now on this ship is under my command. If anyone has a problem with that, speak up."

There was complete silence.

"Then all those with me say 'aye!'" he roared.

"AYE!" came the resounding reply.

So Blackbeard became captain of the ship. Lummocks's crew was far from unhappy about it. In fact, they were relieved to be under the command of a real pirate captain who knew what he was doing.

As for Captain Lummocks, he lay in his cabin, resting his sore ankle, and reading pirate dictionaries to brush up on his bloodthirsty banter. He thought Blackbeard very kind to run his ship while he recovered, and invited him to a roast chicken dinner on his first night. To everyone's surprise, Blackbeard accepted and the two men ate in Lummocks's cabin.

"What kind of pirate *are* you?" Blackbeard asked him, eyeing all the books lining the walls with great suspicion.

"A new one," admitted Lummocks, "who

could use some advice from an old hand. Tell me about the beard. It's legendary and has the most terrifying effect..."

"You like it, eh?" said Blackbeard, flattered. "Well that's the first lesson of piracy. It's all about PRESENCE." Out of his pocket he dug a couple of spare firecrackers. "Fireworks help too," he chortled.

"Oh I see!" laughed Lummocks. Within a few minutes, the two were telling stories and chuckling away like old friends.

"So tell me, what devilish deeds are you up to at the moment?" Lummocks asked.

Blackbeard's eyebrows knitted together. "I'm a-chasin' me tail," he growled. "I've been sailing around trying to find the Seven Seas' treasure." He rummaged in his pockets and brought out a large golden medallion, with lines and lines of numbers engraved on it. "These must be sailing coordinates, but they don't make sense..."

"It could be a code!" exclaimed Lummocks, pointing to an inscription on the back which read:

Ancient changes hold the key,

To the treasure of the Seven Seas.

"Ooh!" he said, rubbing his hands. "Could I try solving it?"

Blackbeard shrugged, "Go on then."

So Lummocks buried his nose in his books. For days, he riffled through pages, scratching his head and making reams of notes. After a week, he called for Blackbeard, bursting with excitement.

"I've cracked it," he blurted when Blackbeard had shut the door behind him. "I've solved the code and worked out where your treasure is. The numbers aren't coordinates. They're page references."

"What the blazes do you mean?" Blackbeard said, scratching his beard. They sat down and Lummocks explained how he'd worked it out.

"'Ancient changes' is code for a very old book named 'Metamorphoses', which means 'changes'. The numbers direct you to pages and words in the book! I've looked them up and worked out the message. Here it is." He pushed a piece of paper, covered in writing, over to Blackbeard.

The fearsome pirate captain rubbed his beard awkwardly, and said, "Can ye read it to me? The thing is... I can't read."

"Can't read?" Lummocks repeated, astounded.

"No," said Blackbeard. "I've always been sort of busy being – you know – frightening..."

"I'll tell you what," Lummocks grinned. "I'll teach you how to read if you can teach me how to be a real pirate captain. Then we'll find the treasure and share it!"

"It's a deal!" Blackbeard agreed.

For the next week, Lummocks and Blackbeard spent every waking hour together in Lummocks's cabin. No one was allowed in; even their meals were left outside the door. Painstakingly, Blackbeard learned to read, first spelling out words, then struggling through sentences. In between, Blackbeard gave Lummocks lessons on how to act like a pirate captain.

The crew had no idea what was going on, but there were some terrible noises coming from the cabin – stammerings that turned into urgent mumbling, and yells that got ever more blood-curdling as the days went by. "'E must be torturing Lummocks to death," said Charlie, wide-eyed. And the idea spread among the crew.

Then, one morning, Captain Blackbeard stuck his head out of the cabin and bellowed, "Avast, you slumbering seasnakes! Plot a course for Rocky Island."

He drew his head back inside. "There's one last lesson you need to learn before you're a real pirate captain," he told Lummocks.

"What's that?" Lummocks asked.

Blackbeard slung a rope around him and tied him to a chair,

gagging him so he couldn't shout for help.

"How to double-cross someone," he laughed. "That treasure's all mine, and after I get it, I'm going to leave you stranded on the island and sail away with your ship. No hard feelings."

Locking the cabin behind him, Blackbeard went to join the crew.

Later that day, Rocky Island loomed into sight. "Alright men, drop anchor. Let's row ashore and dig up that treasure," boomed Blackbeard.

On the beach, the captain dug out Lummocks's notes and led the way, muttering as he read the instructions. "Forty paces north... twelve east... around the

sinking sand... and – ah. Here we are. Dig!"
he ordered the men, pointing between two
jagged rocks.

In no time at all, the crew had uncovered
a treasure chest. They heaved it out of the
sand and cracked it open. The gold lit up
their faces and, as one, they gave a deeply
satisfied, "Arrrr."

They were just rowing back to the ship when there was an earsplitting BOOOOOM! A cannonball crashed into the sea, sending a giant wave crashing over their little boat.

Swaggering around on the deck of the ship was Lummocks. "Avast ye filthy bilge rats!" he yelled down. "Now I have ye scuppered."

"It's a ghost!" wailed Charlie.

"How did you get loose?" growled Blackbeard.

Lummocks rolled his eyes scornfully. "Easy. Lesson five: Always keep a dagger up your sleeve. Now then. Hand over the booty, Blackbeard, or I'll blast ye all to smithereens."

Blackbeard stood up and thundered, "Yer double-crossing scoundrel!"

Lummocks beamed. "Thank you! You told me double-crossing was the last lesson I needed to know to be a real pirate captain. So here I am."

He lowered some buckets over the side of the ship and, grumbling furiously, Blackbeard filled them with the treasure.

"Alright, yer slimy bunch of seamongrels," Lummocks called to his crew. "Everybody who's with me, climb aboard!"

The pirates were so impressed with these newfound dastardly skills, they all swarmed up the side of the ship immediately. Blackbeard was left alone, bobbing on the little boat.

"Shake a leg! Man the rigging! Brace the mainsail!" Lummocks barked, and his crew jumped at his command. As the ship sailed out to sea, the captain turned back to Blackbeard. "See you on the high seas, matey," he yelled. "No hard feelings!"

Captain Strong's Grandma

Captain Strong was a rough, tough pirate, with arms like sides of ham and a chin like a steel shovel. Pirates looked up to him, merchants fled from him. Only this morning, he'd raided six galleons full of gold. To celebrate, he'd docked his ship and gone out to buy a feast.

173

The gangplank bent under the weight of all the yummy grub. "This should keep us going till dinnertime," Strong declared.

As he strode back across the gangplank for the rest of the food, he heard a shrill voice on the wind.

"Cooeee, Wilberforce!"

Strong looked up. "That's odd," he thought. No one called him Wilberforce anymore. No one except...

"Oh no!" he groaned, looking at the little old lady on the quayside. "It's my grandma." He turned bright red and looked for somewhere to hide.

"Are you afraid of your own grandma, Captain?" giggled Lefty, his first mate.

"It's not that," said Captain Strong. "I haven't seen her for years. She doesn't know I'm a pirate..."

"I thought it was you, Wilberforce," said Grandma Strong, tottering towards him. "I'd recognize that face anywhere," she added, tickling the captain under his chin.

"Um, hello Grandma," said Captain Strong, a blush spreading over his cheeks.

"Are you a sailor on this lovely big ship?" asked Grandma Strong.

"He's the captain, ma'am," explained Lefty.

"Ooh, just think... my little Wilberforce, a ship's captain," said Grandma Strong with delight.

"Um, yes," said the captain, thinking quickly. "This is a cruise ship. We take tourists along the coast."

"Well that's just what we've been looking for," said Grandma Strong excitedly.

"*We?*" queried the captain.

"Why yes," replied his grandma. "This way!" she called to a long line of children standing on the quayside.

In a flash, the children trooped across the gangplank and onto the ship, almost knocking the captain and Lefty into the water.

"I help out at the local school,"

explained Grandma Strong. "We're on a day trip, and I thought a cruise along the coast would be very educational."

"B..b..but..." stammered the captain.

"Not too long, mind," said Grandma Strong, following the schoolchildren. "We have to be back by three o'clock."

As Grandma Strong and her class gathered on deck, the captain's crew marched up to him.

"Who are these kids?" cried Scarface.

"I went to sea to get away from children!" moaned Bruiser.

"It's bad luck to bring little old ladies aboard," wailed Crusher.

"Calm down, men," whispered Captain

Strong, and he explained the situation.
"We'll just have to pretend we're a cruise
ship. A quick trip along the coast and they'll
be out of our hair."

"I don't like it," said Bruiser.

"We'll be the laughing stock of the
Pirates' Union," agreed Scarface.

"Just do as you're told, you mangy
bunch," growled Strong. "I'm still the
captain remember?"

With much grumbling, the crew set sail.
Soon *The Mighty Mussel* was out of the
port and sailing along the coast.

Gripping the ship's wheel, Captain
Strong was determined to do the trip in
record time.

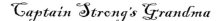

Just then, he felt something
tugging at his sleeve.

"Hey mister," said a tiny voice.
Strong looked down to see a
small boy staring up at him.

"Let go, you little..."
began Strong, before
spotting his grandma
close by. "Um, what
is it, lad?"

"Why have you
got a skull and
crossbones on your
flag?" asked the boy.

"Oh yes," said
Grandma Strong.

"Isn't that a pirate flag?"

"Um, no," said the captain. "It's to show we've got a first aid kit on board."

The little boy didn't look convinced.

"What are these big black things?" cried a girl, pointing to a pile of cannonballs.

"They look like..." began Grandma Strong.

"They're bowling balls, Grandma," interrupted the captain quickly. "For deck games."

"They're a lot heavier than the ones at my bowling club," said Grandma Strong, straining to pick one up.

Just then, a cry went up from the crow's nest.

"Ship ahoy!"

The captain peered through his telescope.

"Oh no!" he whispered to Lefty. "It's *The Black Crab*!"

Deadeye, the captain of *The Black Crab,* was Strong's biggest rival, and the only pirate who'd ever come close to beating him.

Moments later, Deadeye's vessel was alongside *The Mighty Mussel.*

When he saw Grandma Strong and her class on deck, Deadeye couldn't believe it.

"You're recruiting your crew young these days, Strong!" shouted Deadeye, roaring with laughter.

"Ha ha! Very funny!" replied Strong politely, through gritted teeth.

"Do you know my grandson, young man?" asked Grandma Strong.

"Grandson?" chuckled Deadeye. "Do you need your grandma to help you raid merchant ships these days, Strong?"

"I'll see you around, Mr. Deadeye," shouted Strong, trying to steer the ship away.

"Sooner than you think," yelled the other pirate. "I heard you're full of gold booty – but not for long."

With a blood-curdling cry, Deadeye swung across from his ship.

"Grab him, lads!" cried Strong, turning to his crew. But to his horror, he saw that Lefty and the others were lying on the deck, bound and gagged. Standing over them were

Deadeye's men.

"You've been ambushed!" chortled Deadeye. "There's no escape now." He fired his pistol in the air. "Bring me that gold!" he shouted to his crew.

Deadeye's men barged across the deck, scattering children in all directions. Strong's crew was powerless to stop them.

"Out of my way, Grandma," shouted

Deadeye, shoving Grandma Strong aside. "Your grandson's gold is mine for the taking!"

"That's what you think, sonny," she snapped, turning to the children. "Class!" she shouted. "Battle stations!"

At Grandma Strong's command, the children scuttled towards Deadeye's men.

"Waah!" cried one pirate, as a boy leaped up and clung to his face, while a girl wound some rope around his ankles. When the pirate tried to move, he fell to the deck with a thud.

"Wooah!" screamed a group of pirates, as three girls rolled a stream of cannonballs along the deck, toppling them like ninepins.

Captain Strong's Grandma

186

A boy up in the rigging untied a rope, and a huge sail came whooshing down on half a dozen more of Deadeye's men.

"Help!" came their muffled cries. "We can't see."

"You useless worms!" roared Deadeye, as his crew fell like flies around him. "They're just a bunch of kids and a weak old woman."

"Who are you calling weak?" demanded Grandma Strong, grabbing her grandson's telescope and whacking Deadeye in the tummy.

"Ooof!" moaned the pirate, keeling over at her feet.

Grandma Strong and the children quickly helped Captain Strong release his men.

"Nice work, Mrs. Strong!" said Crusher, as he and Bruiser tied up Deadeye's dazed and bewildered crew.

"Congratulations, kids," added Scarface. "You'll make top pirates when you grow up."

"Well that's the idea, dearie," said the old lady.

"What do you mean, Grandma?" asked the captain, who was still in shock.

"Didn't I mention it, Wilberforce?" said Grandma Strong innocently. "I teach at the Puddleby Academy for Junior Pirates. I used to be a pirate before you were born, you know."

"You were a pirate?" gasped her grandson.

"I was one of the roughest, toughest

pirates on the high seas," replied Grandma
Strong. "Just like you," she added, with
a wink.

Pirate Stew

Broadbeard Ben, captain of *The Golden Locust*, was taking his morning stroll on deck when he tripped over a fallen sail.

"Ouch!" said the sail.

"What's that?" cried the captain.

"A stowaway! Come out of there, you toe-stubbing scallywag!"

He whipped off the sail to reveal a small, skinny boy.

"I'm Robin," said the boy. "And I want to join your crew."

"Ha!" laughed Captain Broadbeard. "Only the roughest, toughest, cleverest pirates sail on *The Golden Locust*. And you don't look much tougher than a slouching sea cucumber."

"I'll pass any test you set me," said Robin stoutly. "I'm determined to be a pirate."

"Very well," said the captain. "I have a challenge for you. Let's see if you can make our pirate stew. If you succeed by suppertime, you can join the crew. Alright lad," he added, turning to the helmsman.

Pirate Stew

"Head for Danger Island."

As *The Golden Locust* sailed into a sheltered bay, Captain Broadbeard clapped Robin on the back. "Everything you need to make pirate stew is on this here island," he said, and handed Robin an old map, showing all the ingredients he needed to find.

"Good luck," muttered Captain Broadbeard. "You'll need it!"

Robin slung his bag across his back and set off across the island. "I can do this," he thought. "I'll be a pirate by suppertime."

Soon, he heard the rustle and chatter of monkeys overhead. "Monkey Grove," he realized excitedly. But when he tried to climb the nearest tree, three jabbering monkeys jumped on his head and sent him tumbling to the ground.

"Hey!" cried Robin. Annoyed, he stuck out his tongue. The monkeys in the trees stuck out theirs. Robin jumped and waved his arms. The monkeys jumped and waved right back.

"I've got it," said
Robin. "You imitate
everything I do!" As
the monkeys looked on,
Robin picked up a stone and
tossed it into the air. The
monkeys copied by grabbing
the coconuts and tossing *them* into the air.

Coconuts rained down
around Robin's feet and, in
minutes, he had filled
half his bag.

"Easy!" he
said. "Next
stop, Steep
Sea Cliff..."

"Ah…" he said, when he got there. "This could be a little more tricky."

The cliff, at the very edge of a forest, wasn't just steep. It was sheer. And the gulls' eggs were perched halfway down, on a jutting, narrow ledge.

"I can't climb down that," thought Robin, going trembly at the knees.

Then he spotted a long vine trailing down from the branches of the forest trees. The next moment, he'd tied the vine around his waist and… "Wheee!"

196

He was swinging down the face of the cliff. He stretched out his hands, grabbed the gulls' eggs as he flew past, then abseiled down the rest of the cliff.

"I did it! I did it!" cried Robin, and he carefully placed the eggs in his bag, before looking at the map. "Now for the Forbidden Swamp. How hard can it be to catch a goldfish?"

It wasn't far to the swamp, but Robin trudged for hours through soggy, boggy ponds without finding a single fish.

"It must be getting late," he thought at last. "I'll never be back in time at this rate."

He pulled out his golden pocket watch to check the time – and, as it flashed in the sun, a green torpedo with enormous teeth exploded from the water. It made straight for the watch, gnashing its fearsome jaws. A moment later, the fish splashed back into the swamp, taking a chunk of watch with it.

"Argh!" shouted Robin, scrambling into a tree. "That is not the goldfish I was expecting! But now I know how to catch it."

He pulled off his belt. Using the hook of the buckle, he dangled his golden watch over the bubbling swamp and waited.

Soon, in a flurry of gleaming red fins, another fish shot out of the water, snapping its jaws tightly shut on the golden bait.

"Got you!" crowed Robin, hauling up his vicious prize.

The sun was starting to set over Danger
Island as Robin raced back to *The Golden
Locust*. The crew was ready with a cauldron
of boiling water, bubbling away over a fire.
Robin dropped in his ingredients. The
coconuts were as hard as cannonballs and

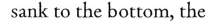

sank to the bottom, the
gulls' eggs were rotten
and the fish fins coated
the cauldron with a
slimy goo.

"Shuddering sharks,"
said Robin as the pirates gathered around.
"That can't be right."

As he spoke, Captain Broadbeard
shouldered his way through the crowd. He

scooped up a scummy, foul-smelling ladle of stew and took a long, deep sniff. "Do you know why we call this pirate stew?" he asked. "Because only a true pirate can make it. You have to be quick, clever and brave — and you've made the best batch of pirate stew I've ever seen. You can join our crew."

"Hurray!" cried Robin, punching the air. Then he looked down at the nutty, eggy, fishy, stinky, slimy mixture in the cauldron. "Now do we have to, um... eat it?" he asked.

The captain laughed. "To be honest," he said, "pirate stew tastes absolutely disgusting. Let's all have ice cream instead."

The
Captain's Cat

Captain Blackheart's ship was the terror of
the seas. With his superb swordfighting
skills and unflagging appetite for treasure,
no other pirate could match
him. He had just one
small secret. Blackheart,
the most fearsome pirate
of all, was terrified of...

mice! Rats, cockroaches, cutlass-wielding enemies, Blackheart could take in his stride. But one glimpse of a twitching pink nose and his tummy turned somersaults.

Being afraid of mice isn't good for a pirate. If Blackheart's crew or enemies found out, he'd be laughed out of a job.

For this reason, he never set sail without his cat, Biscuit. Though Biscuit loved nothing better than a long, peaceful nap, when he wasn't snoozing, he was a champion mouser. With Biscuit on board, no mouse dared show its face, leaving Blackheart free to plunder and pillage and generally be the most dastardly pirate around.

One day, Blackheart and his crew

captured a trading ship loaded with fine
fabrics and fancy clothes. While the rest
of the crew tried on frilly petticoats and
flowery hats and roared with laughter,
Blackheart spotted a chest full of gleaming
jewels, silks and furs. "I'll have that one,"
he barked, hefting it back to his cabin.

Biscuit purred when he saw the chest.
He thought it looked like a perfect place for
a nap. So as Blackheart sat down to sharpen
his cutlass, he jumped in and curled up
comfortably inside.

Meanwhile, beady eyes were
spying on Blackheart's
ship from afar. It's hard
to be a successful

pirate without other pirates eyeing up your loot enviously. Other pirates like Samuel Sly...

"Blackheart has stolen more gold and jewels than anyone," Sly told his crew. "I bet he keeps the best pieces in his cabin, where no one can get 'em – no one except me!" he added proudly. For if Blackheart was the most ferocious pirate afloat, Sly was undoubtedly the sneakiest.

That night, while Blackheart and his crew guzzled down a dinner of delicious fish stew, a dark shape swam silently up to the ship. Stealthy fingers gripped the anchor chain, climbed up and pushed open a porthole...

"I made it!" thought Sly in delight, as he

gazed around the
captain's cabin. "Now,
where's that treasure?"
His eyes lighted greedily
on a wooden chest.
"That must be it!"
Quickly, he hefted it
onto his shoulder
and tiptoed away.

When Blackheart got back to his cabin,
there was no chest, only a trail of wet
footprints. He had no doubt who was to
blame. "Samuel Sly!" he hissed. "That
scurvy bilge rat. No one else would dare to
steal from *me!*"

A thought struck him. *Biscuit?* The cat

had been curled up inside the chest. Now the chest was gone. He turned pale as the awful truth dawned. His cat was gone too.

"What's the matter, Cap'n?" asked Dan, the second-in-command, poking his head around the door.

"We've been robbed," wailed Blackheart. "My chest... Samuel Sly has taken it!"

Dan laughed. "He'll get a surprise when he finds it's mostly clothes."

"Never mind that," snapped Blackheart. "I've got to get it back..."

Just then, something darted past outside. Something small, with a wiggling tail.

"Ugh!" Blackheart yelped.

"Are you all right?" asked Dan

suspiciously.

"Um, fine," said Blackheart quickly. "Just clearing my throat. *Co-ugh, co-ugh!* I seem to be getting a cold. I'd better stay in my cabin while you give the order to set sail."

As soon as Dan had left, he slammed the door and began hunting feverishly for mousetraps. "The little vermin must have been in the cargo we stole today!"

It didn't take long to reach Samuel Sly's hideout. In a narrow cove, a dirty-looking ship with ragged sails bobbed at anchor.

Blackheart opened a porthole and glared through his telescope. The deck of Sly's ship was littered with old boxes and sacks of rotting cabbages. And there, right in the middle of it all, was the missing chest.

As he looked, something scurried out from behind a heap of cabbage leaves. *Pitter-patter. Pitter-patter.* Something small, scratching and scrabbling...

"*Aaaaaaaargh!*" he screeched. There were mice *everywhere.*

"Is that cold still bothering you?" asked Dan, coming in.

"*Aaaa-tish-oo!*" said Blackheart hurriedly. "Um, maybe." He thought about the mice and gritted his teeth. He had to get Biscuit back before his own ship was overrun. He took a deep breath... stood up as tall as he could, grabbed his cutlass and marched out on deck. "Let's fight!"

"Aye, aye, sir!" said Dan, giving a fierce, gap-toothed grin.

They steered alongside Sly's ship and Blackheart raised his weapon high in the air.

"ATTACK!" he yelled, hoping his voice wouldn't tremble. Then he seized a rope, stuck his cutlass between his teeth and swung across to the enemy deck.

Within moments, the sound of steel on steel filled the air, as cutlasses clashed and daggers were drawn. Driven on by fear, Blackheart fought his way over to Sly.

"You pox-faced, sneaking swine," yelled Blackheart, towering over his opponent.

"Ha! You're nothing but a lily-livered worm," snarled Sly.

The Captain's Cat

Scowling, Blackheart raised his cutlass –
and then it happened. A mouse dashed
between them, diving for cover behind Sly.

"*Aaaaaaaaaaaaaargh,*" screamed
Blackheart again, waving the cutlass wildly.
"Get away, you filthy little vermin!"

He screamed so loudly, all the other
pirates stopped fighting and turned to look.
Sly's jaw dropped.

For a moment, Blackheart saw his career
slipping away from him. "Now everyone
knows," he thought miserably. "They'll never
stop laughing at me."

But Sly saw the most fearsome pirate on
the seven seas, brandishing an enormous
cutlass and yelling like a madman. His face

turned white and his sword fell from his
fingers. Then he turned and ran, diving into
the sea in his haste to get away.

The mouse stayed where it
was, sniffing the air.
Blackheart gulped. But
before he could move,
there was a fierce yowl.
Then an orange blur sped
across the deck, and the mouse ran for it.

"Biscuit!" cried Blackheart
in delight.

The noise of fighting had finally
woken the cat from his nap, and he set
about doing what he did best. Blackheart
watched happily as Biscuit caught mouse

214

after mouse after mouse.

And when Sly surfaced, spitting seaweed, all the pirates were laughing at *him* – Blackheart loudest of all.

"Never steal from a fellow pirate," he chuckled as he took back his chest, Biscuit draped happily around his shoulders. "Especially when it comes to his cat!"

The Rescue Plan

"That was the best pirate party ever," declared Fred Wimple, swaying gently on his hammock.

Across the ship's deck, Sam Flint swept up the mess from the party —

burst balloons, broken tankards and
snapped wooden legs caused by a crash in
the three-legged race.

Sam and Fred loved pirate parties. Ever
since their captain, Mad Mac Macgregor, had
been arrested, they had been free to party all
the time. Last night's party was the best yet,
with pin the tail on the mermaid, sea-shanty
karaoke and an epic pirate jig dance-off.

But, that morning, something nagged at
Sam. He felt as if he'd forgotten something.

"Look at this," said Fred.

Fred sat up, showing off a hat decorated
with tiny Jolly Rogers and so many feathers
that Sam wondered if some poor parrot in
the port had been plucked bare.

"I stole it from Two Hook Tim when he was dunking for doubloons." Fred chuckled, lying back in his hammock. "Pirate parties are the best parties."

"Fred," Sam asked, "are we supposed to be doing something today?"

"Sleeping," Fred replied. "Peg Leg Pat is having a party later. We can't miss it. There might be musical chairs... charades..."

"Charades..." Sam gasped, as he remembered. Yesterday they'd visited Captain Macgregor in jail, and played charades through the bars of his cell. After some confusion, Sam had realized the captain was secretly acting out an escape plan, to save him from the gallows.

Sam recalled the captain's whispered warning. "If you don't save me, I'll come back to haunt you."

"We're supposed to be at the town square at twelve o'clock today to save Captain Macgregor!" he said. "How could we forget the rescue plan?"

"How *could* we?" Fred said. "It was a brilliant plan. Hang on, what was it?"

"It involved a parrot," Sam said.

"And an electric eel," Fred muttered.

"And a glass eyeball. Definitely a glass eyeball."

Sam pelted down the gangplank. "Come on," he said. "We've got ten minutes to find all those things and save the captain."

"Is there time for breakfast first?" Fred said, following.

As he ran, his party hat slid over his eyes causing him to trip and tumble into Sam. They crashed onto the dock beside a stall selling fishing nets, treasure chests and birds in cages.

"Parrots!" Sam said. "But we spent all our money on party decorations. We'll have to steal one."

He waited until the stall owner wasn't looking, and then lifted one of the cages from its hook.

"DIRTY THIEF!" squawked the parrot. "DIRTY THIEF! DIRTY THIEF!"

"Run!" Fred cried.

Sam gripped the cage and they ran from the dock. They hid in an alley as the stall owner charged past.

"All right," Sam wheezed. "Now we need an electric eel and a glass eyeball. But time's running out to save Captain Macgregor. What do we do?"

"Have breakfast?" Fred suggested.

"This is serious, Fred! Captain Macgregor will haunt us for the *rest of our lives*. We'll never be invited to a party again, not with a ghost floating beside us. Remember how the captain always said we were useless, cowardly pirates. Well, now we can prove him wrong. We have to think as we've never thought before. Where can we find an electric eel?"

Fred scratched his chin. Picked his nose. Tilted his pirate party hat to a jaunty angle.

"Any ideas?" Sam said.

"About what?"

"Arrgh! About the eel."

"I can't think when I'm this hungry," Fred moaned. "I need one of Warty Wendy's eel pies."

"Fred that's it! Come on."

They raced along twisting lanes, to a strip of rickety wooden shops with greasy windows and creaking signs. The creakiest sign said:

The door opened with a groan. Sam covered his nose, revolted by the reek of rotten eel from inside. Splodges of gravy and mushy peas puddled the floor.

Behind the counter, Warty Wendy

watched them approach. She only had one wart, but it was right on the end of her finger. It was white with a black tip, and looked like a tiny glaring eyeball.

"Whadaya want?" she snapped, wiggling the wart at them.

"An electric eel," Sam said, edging back.

The wart seemed to widen, and a gasp came from Wendy's lips. "The only pirates that want an electric eel are those planning to rescue someone from hanging," she said.

"No," Sam said. "We want it for... a pet. Ain't that right, Fred?"

"Yes. I love electric eels. Their funny little faces."

"He keeps them on his shoulder," Sam

added. "Like other pirates do with parrots."

Warty Wendy grabbed a jar from under the counter and thumped it down on the surface. Inside, a slimy eel wriggled in dirty water. "Let's see you do that then," she said.

Sam gripped Fred's arm. "You have to do it," he whispered. "We've only got five minutes, and we need that eel."

Groaning, Fred slid his fingers inside the jar. His hand shook as he lifted the slippery creature out, and put it on his shoulder.

"It's actually quite cute," he said. "Hey, why is it called an 'electric' eel?"

ZAAAP!

There was a crackle of blue light, and Fred jumped in the air. Wisps of smoke rose

The Rescue Plan

from the top of his pirate party hat. "Yaaa!" he cried, and then "Yaaa!" again as the eel zapped him with another electric shock.

Tossing the creature from hand to hand, he ran after Sam and out of the shop. His shrieks rang around the walls as the eel zapped him again and again.

"How long –YAAA! – do we have – YAAA! – to save – YAAA! – Captain Macgregor?"

"Four minutes," Sam said, ducking down another alley. "But we still don't have a glass eyeball."

"Uh, Sam? That's not our only problem..."

A dark figure blocked the end of the alley. A pirate with two hooks for hands.

"It's Two Hook Tim," Fred breathed, dragging Sam behind some barrels to hide.

"Fred Wimple!" the pirate roared. "You stole my pirate party hat."

He scraped one hook hand against the other, sharpening them like knives. "I've been shot at by the army, keelhauled by the navy and cursed by a witch. But no one ever dared steal my party hat."

Two Hook Tim stomped closer. Sunlight caught his eyes, and one of them glinted.

"A glass eye!" Sam said. "We have to get it, Fred. We'll prove to Captain Macgregor that we can be brave pirates. Are you ready?"

"No."

"That's the spirit. CHARGE!"

They burst from behind the barrels and ran at Two Hook Tim.

Sam screamed, "Give us your eye!" and Fred shrieked, "Please don't hurt me!" and the parrot squawked and the eel filled the alley with bursts of livid blue light.

Two Hook Tim's mouth hung open in horror. A long time ago, a witch had put a curse on him, swearing that he would meet his end at the hands of two pirates with a parrot and an electric eel. He wasn't taking any chances.

He plucked out his glass eyeball, dropped it to the ground, then turned and fled. "Keep the hat too," he yelled.

Sam snatched up the eye and stumbled out into the town square. The town hall clock said two minutes to twelve.

"Argh!" cried Sam. "How are we supposed to *use* the parrot, the eel and the glass eyeball? We'll never be able to come up with a rescue plan in two minutes."

"Um... hang on," said Fred. "Where is everyone?"

A mangy dog scurried across the cobbles, and a criminal sat miserably in the stocks. Otherwise, the square was empty.

"Hey," Sam asked the criminal. "Isn't Captain Macgregor due at twelve o'clock?"

"Aye," the criminal said. "Twelve o'clock tomorrow."

"Tomorrow?" Fred cried. "Hooray! There's still time to make a plan. The captain was wrong. We've proved we can be brave pirates. We'll tell him when we rescue him tomorrow."

The Rescue Plan

Sam's smile grew wider. "But first..."

"Peg Leg Pat's party!" they said together.

The Curse of the Black Parrot

Every pirate wanted to be a member of
Captain Clover's crew. He was the luckiest
pirate who ever set sail. The old sea dog had
raided over fifty galleons, and never
been caught.

Some people (usually the captain) said it was because of his expert pirating skills. Others thought he hypnotized his opponents.

Whatever the reason, pirates lined the docks to join up whenever there was a job aboard Clover's ship, *The Jolly Lobster.*

Tom had come aboard as a cabin boy almost a year ago, and was looking forward to yet another lucky voyage.

"Ship ahoy!" came a cry from the crow's nest. Tom joined the rest of the crew as they scrambled on deck to catch a glimpse of their next target.

But instead of sailing away from the pirates, as most sensible ships did, this one was heading straight for them.

As it got closer, Captain Clover's face went as white as a skull and crossbones.

"Oh no!" he yelped, nervously stroking Percy, his faithful black parrot, who sat perched on his shoulder as always.

"What's the matter, Captain?" asked Tom.

"It's *The Grim Squid*," explained Clover nervously. "That can only mean..."

"That's right!" roared a voice like a rusty saw, and a ragged, filthy pirate swung across from the other ship. Without setting foot on deck, he swooped down, plucked Percy from the captain's shoulder and swung back to his own ship.

"Who was that?" cried Tom.

"That was Ruthless Rufus," wailed the

captain. "He's stolen Percy and now we're done for!"

Tom had never seen the captain so miserable. He knew Clover was fond of his parrot, but he couldn't see why he was quite so depressed.

As *The Grim Squid* sailed away, with Ruthless Rufus's laughter drifting in the breeze, Captain Clover slumped down on the deck with his head in his hands.

"You may as well know the truth!" he moaned, as his crew gathered around. "It wasn't because of me that we've been so lucky over the years. It was thanks to Percy."

"How could that be?" asked Tom.

"It all started many years ago," explained the captain. "Rufus and I had just graduated from The Crooked Claw Pirate Training School. We were on our way to the docks to steal our first ships, when we came across an old woman sitting by the roadside.

'Can you help me home, sailors?' she asked. 'I got a stone stuck in my boot and now my foot is too sore to walk on.'

Rufus just laughed. 'Tough tadpoles, grandma!' he cried and strolled on. But I felt sorry for the old lady. So I agreed to give her a piggyback ride to the dockside inn.

When we arrived, Rufus had been stuffing his face with pies for the past hour.

It was then the woman told us she was a witch. 'Let me reward you,' she said, and handed me a tiny black egg.

'Take good care of that egg,' she said. 'By midnight it will hatch into a black parrot. That bird will bring good fortune to whoever owns it.'

'Codswallop!' roared Rufus. But I had faith in the old woman. Sure enough the egg hatched, and that black parrot brought me good luck from that day to this."

"Rufus must have heard about how lucky you've been, and come after Percy," said Tom.

"We'll never get him back," sniffed Clover. "I know Rufus. He'll keep poor Percy under lock and key day and night."

"Maybe we can persuade him to give Percy back," said Tom, thoughtfully.

"Never!" said Clover in despair.

"Let me see," Tom went on. "I'll need a bottle, some rats and lamp oil, and then I'll have to sneak onto their ship..."

The next morning, the crew of *The Grim*

Squid woke to hear a thud, thud, thud against the hull.

"What's that racket?" bellowed Ruthless Rufus, hurling a bucket at Snivel, the first mate.

"Look Captain!" cried Snivel. "It's a bottle, floating in the water. And there's a piece of paper inside."

"It could be money!" cried Rufus eagerly. "Now I've got that parrot, anything's possible. Bring it aboard."

"Is it money?" asked Snivel, as the captain tugged the paper from the bottle.

"Better than that," smirked Rufus. "It's a treasure map. According to this, there's a fortune buried on Lonesome Island."

The crew's eyes lit up with greed.

"Full sail for Lonesome Island!" ordered Rufus.

An hour later, *The Grim Squid* was anchored off shore.

"Bring every shovel we have!" barked Rufus to his crew as they climbed into a little boat. "I'll bring the bird," he added, swinging a rusty bird cage containing Percy. "The closer the luck is, the more treasure we're likely to dig up."

They rowed across to the island and jumped ashore.

"Ow!" yelled Rufus, as a giant crab popped out of the sand and nipped his foot.

"Yow!" shrieked Snivel, as another crab

pinched him on the bottom.

The injured pirates ran into the jungle to escape. But it wasn't long before they were bitten red raw by hundreds of buzzing bugs.

"Get off!" cried Snivel, swatting the air.

"Darn these munching marauders!" cursed Rufus.

With the bugs swarming after them, the pirates scrambled into a steamy swamp.

They slipped and slithered along, and soon found themselves sinking into squelching mud.

"I'm stuck!" wailed Snivel.

"Suffering sand eels!" roared Rufus, lifting his wooden leg from the slimy goo.

Puffing and panting, they dragged

The Curse of the Black Parrot

themselves on, until at last they reached the place marked on the map with a cross.

"Alright, you barnacles," puffed Rufus. "Start digging!"

The crew dug down and down and down. They sweated away for ten hours, but all they got for their trouble were blisters and backaches.

"So much for the lucky parrot," moaned Snivel. "There's nothing there."

"Quiet!" shouted Rufus, shooting an angry look at Percy. "We'll come back tomorrow and keep looking."

The exhausted pirates limped back to the shore and rowed across to their ship.

"I'm starving!" yelled Rufus. "Bring out

the ship's biscuits."

Snivel rolled a big barrel across the deck. The captain tore off the lid and reached inside.

"Agggh!" he yelped. He whipped out his hand as a dozen rats scrabbled out, one with its teeth embedded in his finger. The rats scuttled across the ship.

"They've eaten all the biscuits," moaned Snivel, surveying the crumbs at the bottom of the barrel. "That's not what I call luck."

"Silence!" boomed Rufus, glowering at Percy from the corner of his eye. "Fetch me some grog, Snivel, I'm parched."

Dodging the filthy rats, Snivel went to the barrel and filled the captain's tankard.

"I've been looking forward to this all day," said Rufus, licking his lips.

"Bleuurrgh!" he spluttered, spitting a mouthful across the deck. "That's disgusting! It tastes like oil."

"It's all that parrot's fault!" wailed Snivel.

"We've had nothing but bad luck since he came aboard," cried another pirate.

At that moment, *The Jolly Lobster* appeared alongside.

"Ahoy there!" shouted Captain Clover.

"Hope you like your new pet, Rufus," he laughed.

Rufus grabbed the bird cage and flung it across to the other ship.

"You can keep your dratted bird!" he growled. "The wretched thing's cursed."

Clover released Percy from the cage and popped him back on his shoulder. "Cursed for you," he called to Rufus. Then he turned to his parrot. "But lucky for me," he said with a smile.

The Pirate Prince

Once upon a time, there was a handsome prince named Rafi, who was about to be married to a princess from a faraway land. Princess Sophia was said to be the most beautiful woman in the world, although Rafi had never actually *seen* her. All he had was a portrait.

In the painting, she had a haughty expression, and a fluffy little dog under her arm. Rafi hated fluffy little dogs.

"What's the point of a dog you can't take hunting?" he thought. "And look at that dress! So pink and frilly! Yuck!"

No, Rafi did not want to marry Princess Sophia. He wanted to have adventures.

"And don't even *think* of trying to get out of it," said his mother, the night before the wedding. Rafi was trying on his gold silk outfit. It itched like a plague of fire ants.

"Most princes would be thrilled to be in your shoes," his mother went on.

Prince Rafi looked down at his shoes, which were pointed and shiny and very uncomfortable. "They can have my shoes," he muttered.

That evening, he decided to run away. As dusk fell, Rafi changed into his oldest clothes and glanced at the portrait of Princess Sophia, mouthing, "Sorry," before he climbed out of the window.

Rafi rode as hard and fast as he could to the sea. *Where better to have adventures?* He rode all night, and in the morning, he reached a busy port.

The first vessel he saw was a pirate ship, called *The Night King*. Rafi laughed with joy. "A pirate ship! What could be better? No one has more adventures than pirates!"

A small woman with white hair and stern

black eyes came over to him. "Yes?" she said, roughly, giving him a poke in the chest. "Who are you and what do you want?"

Rafi was taken aback. People usually simpered when they met him and showered him with flattery. He wasn't used to someone being so blunt. He decided that he rather liked it.

"My name's Rafi," he said. "And I'd like a job on this ship."

"Hmm... Well, I'm its captain, Captain Beefheart," replied the woman, looking him up and down. "You look strong enough to be a pirate. But can you fight?"

Rafi nodded eagerly. "I've been training since my ninth birthday," he said.

It was perfectly true. As part of his princely lessons, he'd learned to handle all kinds of weapons.

The captain clapped him on the back and ushered him up the gangplank. "Good! Then you can start as cabin boy immediately. We could do with new blood on board. Set sail, me hearties!"

The pirate crew shouted, "Yes Ma'am!" and pushed off from the docks.

"Where are we going?" asked Rafi.

"To fight, my lad," said the captain. "Captain Pox of the *The Mermaid's Curse* stole my treasure last week. We're going to get it back!"

Rafi's eyes widened. *A real pirate battle!* He hadn't expected quite so much adventure all at once. He couldn't believe his luck.

They sailed all day without any sign of the enemy, then feasted that night. The other pirates told Rafi tales of a pirate named Slice.

"She's just joined *The Mermaid's Curse* and no one knows her real name," said Captain Beefheart. "She's new to these seas but fights more fiercely than ten men. She wears a jet-black mask and an inky-blue cloak and her sword shines like the moon."

The pirates all shivered and muttered. "I don't want to have to fight her again," said one. "I barely escaped with my life."

Rafi laughed. "I'm not afraid," he said. "I'll take her on."

The pirates all raised their glasses. "May your blade be as bold as your boast," said the captain.

When Rafi went to bed that night, in a hammock in the hold, he slept better than he ever had in his soft palace bed. Rocked to sleep by the ocean, he dreamed of single combat with the mysterious pirate Slice.

A great clashing from up on deck yanked him out of his dreams. "We're under attack!" someone cried. "*The Mermaid's Curse* has ambushed us. The crew heard we were coming to get them and they're attacking *us* instead!"

Rafi quickly climbed up the ladder, grabbing his sword as he went. In the early morning light, he saw that the deck was full of stomping, wrestling, sword-waving, grimacing pirates.

He started forward, excited. *If Slice is really on board, I can show my crew that I'm the greatest pirate in these parts!*

Rafi's grand thoughts were interrupted when someone kicked him in the stomach. He staggered and bent double, but he didn't lose hold of his sword.

His attacker was a young woman, about Rafi's own age, with brown, tousled hair and dark brown eyes. She wore a black mask and a dark cloak, and her blade glinted in the rising sun. She lunged at him with her sword, and he parried, in spite of the pain in his bruised belly.

"I'm Slice," said the girl, as sword clashed on sword.

"I thought so," said Rafi. "But I thought you'd be bigger, from the stories they tell of you."

"From the stories *no one* tells of you, I didn't think of you *at all,*" Slice snarled. She swung her sword in a whistling arc. Rafi leaped back, and the blade missed his chest by a whisker.

"I don't need stories," said Rafi, "when I have skill."

"Oh really? Where?" said Slice, and lunged again.

By this time, Rafi was dimly aware that he had an audience. Pirates from both ships were standing in a circle around them as they fought. Next to Captain Beefheart stood a brown-bearded man in a captain's hat.

"Go Rafi!" cried Captain Beefheart. "You can beat Captain Pox's lass easily!"

"Get him, Slice," cried the other captain. "Show him *The Mermaid's Curse* has the greatest crew on the seven seas!"

"How about a wager, Pox?" hollered Captain Beefheart, over the clash of swords. "If your Slice wins, we'll give you the treasure. But if my Rafi wins, you'll clear off and find your own gold."

"It's a deal!" Captain Pox agreed.

Rafi was too busy to worry about deals and treasure. The only thing he cared about right now was not getting skewered by the sharp sword Slice was thrusting at him.

"Come on, boy," she hissed. "Why are you holding back?"

"I'm not," snapped Rafi.

The Pirate Prince

"Oh dear," said Slice. Her sarcastic smile gave Rafi a new burst of strength.

"YAAAAAAAAAAAAR!" he cried, and ran at her. A flurry of blows passed between them, steel clashing on steel. As Rafi pushed forward, Slice danced back. They moved across the deck, striking again and again, back and forth. The pirates around them roared and cheered and stomped their feet.

Rafi felt a rush of joy as he fought. But then, taking a dancing step back, he stumbled on a coil of rope.

Slice took her chance and lunged. Rafi rolled out from under the slicing steel, staggering to his feet. He blocked her blade as it came down, and their eyes met. Rafi

froze. He'd seen those dark eyes somewhere
before... Slice was staring at him, too.

"Are you..." she said. "Prince Rafi?"

Rafi nodded. "Are you..." he replied.
"Princess Sophia?"

Slice nodded and pulled off her mask.
Princess Sophia, the girl from the painting,
was standing before Rafi. Only instead of

a pink fluffy dress, she wore black, and in place of a yappy little dog, she had a sword. There was no sign of a snooty, simpering smile now – she was covered in sweat and beaming from ear to ear.

They both dropped their swords to the ground with a clatter. Captains Beefheart and Pox looked puzzled.

"What's going on?" demanded Captain Beefheart. "What's this about princes and princesses? I thought this was a pirate ship!"

"It is. We're all pirates here," said Slice. "But I used to be a princess..." She gestured to Rafi, "...and this is the prince I ran away to sea to avoid marrying."

"And I ran away to sea to avoid marrying

her," said Rafi, pointing to Sophia. "Nothing personal," he added. "I just wanted adventure."

"Me too!" said Sophia.

Captain Beefheart and Captain Pox exchanged glances. Then they shrugged.

"Well, well," said Beefheart. "It seems they teach royals how to fight nicely these days," and she clapped Rafi on the back.

The pirates all cheered and Captain Pox declared that, in celebration of this reunion, the two ships would split the treasure. As a raucous pirate party began, Rafi and Slice took a couple of drinks and crept off to a corner.

"You know, you don't look much like

your portrait," said Rafi.

Slice laughed. "That silly little dog isn't even mine, my mother made me pose with him. You don't look much like your picture, either. The painting my mother showed me was of a stuffy young man in a gold suit with a pained expression."

"That gold suit was *really, really* uncomfortable," said Rafi. He looked down at his pirate rags, then raised his glass. "Here's to rags and adventure," he said.

"Aye," said Slice. "I'll drink to that. So why don't we start now?"

"Start what?"

"The adventure," said Slice. She pointed to a little boat that hung on ropes off the side of the ship. "You, me, a stash of weapons and the open sea." She pulled a knife from her boot and gestured at the ropes. "All it takes is one little slice."

She grinned.

Rafi grinned right back.

Being a cabin boy was one thing, but running your own ship – even a tiny one like that – would be even more wonderful.

He did feel a little guilty, however. "Won't the captains be angry if we steal the boat and run away?" asked Rafi.

Slice made a face. "We're pirates. We can do what we want and go where we like!"

So they did. The former Princess Sophia and Prince Rafi sailed away in search of treasure and adventure. "It was," Rafi thought, "love at first fight."

Usborne Quicklinks

For links to websites where you can find fun pirate facts and activities, go to the Usborne Quicklinks website at **www.usborne.com/ quicklinks**, type the keyword "pirates" then click on the title of this book.

Children – please ask an adult before using the internet, and follow the internet safety guidelines displayed at the Usborne Quicklinks website.

The recommended websites at Usborne Quicklinks are regularly reviewed and updated, but Usborne Publishing Ltd. is not responsible for the content or availability of any website other than its own.

We recommend that children are supervised while using the internet.

Acknowledgements

Stories written by:
Rosie Dickins, Rosie Hore, Rob Lloyd Jones,
Jerome Martin, Anna Milbourne,
Russell Punter and Louie Stowell

Edited by Susanna Davidson
and Lesley Sims

Designed by Brenda Cole

Cover design by Stephen Moncrieff
Additional cover design by Zuzanna Bujala

Digital manipulation by Nick Wakeford and John Russell